Match Wits with The Hardy Boys®!

Collect the Original
Hardy Boys Mystery Stories®
by Franklin W. Dixon

The Tower Treasure
The House on the Cliff
The Secret of the Old Mill
The Missing Chums
Hunting for Hidden Gold
The Shore Road Mystery
The Secret of the Caves
The Mystery of Cabin Island
The Great Airport Mystery
What Happened at Midnight
While the Clock Ticked
Footprints Under the Window
The Mark on the Door
The Hidden Harbor Mystery
The Sinister Signpost
A Figure in Hiding
The Secret Warning
The Twisted Claw
The Disappearing Floor
The Mystery of the Flying Express
The Clue of the Broken Blade
The Flickering Torch Mystery
The Melted Coins
The Short-Wave Mystery
The Secret Panel
The Phantom Freighter
The Secret of Skull Mountain
The Sign of the Crooked Arrow
The Secret of the Lost Tunnel
The Wailing Siren Mystery
The Secret of Wildcat Swamp

The Crisscross Shadow
The Yellow Feather Mystery
The Hooded Hawk Mystery
The Clue in the Embers
The Secret of Pirates' Hill
The Ghost at Skeleton Rock
The Mystery at Devil's Paw
The Mystery of the Chinese Junk
Mystery of the Desert Giant
The Clue of the Screeching Owl
The Viking Symbol Mystery
The Mystery of the Aztec Warrior
The Haunted Fort
The Mystery of the Spiral Bridge
The Secret Agent on Flight 101
Mystery of the Whale Tattoo
The Arctic Patrol Mystery
The Bombay Boomerang
Danger of Vampire Trail
The Masked Monkey
The Shattered Helmet
The Clue of the Hissing Serpent
The Mysterious Caravan
The Witchmaster's Key
The Jungle Pyramid
The Firebird Rocket
The Sting of the Scorpion
Hardy Boys Detective Handbook
The Hardy Boys Back-to-Back
    The Tower Treasure/ The House
    on the Cliff

Celebrate 60 Years with the World's Greatest Super Sleuths!

MYSTERY OF THE WHALE TATTOO

ONE exciting event follows another when Frank and Joe Hardy are hired to apprehend the pickpockets who have been plaguing Solo's Super Carnival. When their friends Tony Prito and Biff Hooper exhibit a stuffed whale dug up at a construction project, they all but put the carnival out of business.

Other unforeseen problems ensue when the teen-age sleuths become involved in their father's latest case. Fenton Hardy is tracking down a priceless ivory idol stolen from a Hong Kong art collector. A postcard clue found at the carnival leads Frank and Joe and their buddy Chet Morton to the historic seaport town of Mystic in Connecticut, to a seaman's home in New York City, to a stunning discovery in Los Angeles.

In this thrilling mystery the young detectives pit their wits against a gang of thieves whose bizarre identification, a three-part whale tattoo, proves to be a nearly insolvable riddle.

"Frank!" Joe gasped. *"We'll never make it
with the statue!"*

The Hardy Boys Mystery Stories®

MYSTERY
OF THE
WHALE TATTOO

BY

FRANKLIN W. DIXON

GROSSET & DUNLAP
Publishers • New York
A member of The Putnam & Grosset Group

PRINTED ON RECYCLED PAPER

CONTENTS

MYSTERY
OF THE
WHALE TATTOO

CHAPTER I

Hey Rube!

JOE Hardy studied the photograph in his hand and frowned, then burst out laughing.

"What a weirdo!" exclaimed the blond seventeen-year-old boy. "Take a look at him, Frank!"

He gave the snapshot to his dark-haired brother, who was eighteen. Both boys, sons of Fenton Hardy, the famous private detective, had hurried into the living room at the call of their Aunt Gertrude. She had just opened an envelope which contained the snapshot and a letter.

Frank gazed at the man in the picture. His head was topped with a shock of light-colored hair, and his cheeks and chin were hidden beneath a full, flowing beard.

"Sure is a freak," Frank commented.

"That's not the way to talk about a relative, especially when he's coming to visit," Aunt Gertrude said sternly, trying to hide a smile.

1

She was a tall, sharp-featured woman who wore metal-rimmed spectacles. Her prim visage was deceptive, though, for beneath her forbidding appearance she was really one of the kindest persons one could ever hope to meet.

"A relative?" Joe burst out. "You're kidding!"

"I am not! That's Elmer Hardy, a second cousin to your father and me," their aunt corrected. "Too bad Fenton's not at home," she added.

Mr. Hardy was on a tricky undercover assignment in New York City, where as a young man he had achieved an enviable record on the police force. That was before he had come to Bayport to start his own detective agency. Now Frank and Joe were following in their father's footsteps as astute young sleuths.

The news about Elmer Hardy's proposed visit stirred their curiosity.

"How come we've never heard of him?" Joe asked.

"Well, you see nobody in the family has set eyes on him for thirty years," Aunt Gertrude explained, "ever since the day he ran away to sea. Elmer always was a bit of a wild one."

Frank shook his head. "Thirty years is a long time to go without hearing from someone."

"Oh, we've exchanged a few letters over the years. Right from the start he's had a standing

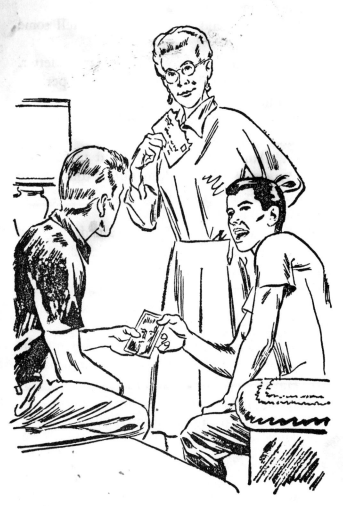

"A relative?" Joe burst out. "You're kidding!"

invitation to come and visit us, and that's just what he's going to do."

"Great!" Joe said. "I'll bet he can tell some terrific sea tales."

Aunt Gertrude consulted Elmer Hardy's letter. "He'll be arriving in about two weeks, perhaps sooner if he can manage it."

"May I keep the picture a while, so I can show it to Chet?" Joe asked.

"Yes," Aunt Gertrude said. "But mind now, you boys get all that laughing out of your system before Elmer arrives." She waggled a finger at them to emphasize her point.

"Yes, ma'am!" Frank and Joe grinned.

The telephone rang. Frank picked it up. "Hello?" His eyes widened. "Just a second, Dad." He put his hand over the mouthpiece. "Joe, Dad's run into some problems. Get on the extension in his study."

Frank waited while his brother raced up the stairs to the second floor. It was highly unusual for Mr. Hardy to contact his family while working undercover and both boys were on the alert.

Joe picked up the extension. "Okay, Dad, go ahead."

"I'll try to make this brief," Mr. Hardy told his sons. "I want you to find someone for me, if it's at all possible. I'll give you the background so listen carefully."

"All right. Shoot!" Joe said.

Fenton Hardy explained that his quest was for a life-sized statue known as the "Ivory Idol," carved in the shape of a six-armed deity during the Ming dynasty. Ten years ago a gang of merchant sailors had stolen the Ivory Idol from the internationally famous Dudley-Harris collection in Hong Kong.

"There were reliable reports," Mr. Hardy said, "that the statue arrived in the United States a few months after its theft, but the police failed to turn up the slightest trace of it."

Frank and Joe jotted down the pertinent bits of information in pocket-sized notebooks, as their father went on, "One month ago R. R. Dunn, the famous New York art collector, received a note saying he could purchase the Ivory Idol for his private collection."

"Wow! So it turned up!" Joe exclaimed.

"Not quite yet. The price is fifty thousand dollars, and the thieves are asking a ten-thousand-dollar advance to cover their 'expenses.'"

"Who sent the note?" Frank asked.

"It's signed *Blackright,* nothing more," Mr. Hardy answered.

The detective went on to say that R. R. Dunn, as an honest collector, had notified Mr. Dudley-Harris immediately. The latter called the police and also engaged the services of Mr. Hardy.

"Any clues so far?" Joe inquired impatiently.

"Yes. An informer contacted the police last night and said that he knew something about

Blackright. But the price he asked for his information was too high. Furthermore, he wanted a huge reward if Blackright was apprehended."

"Quite a wheeler-dealer!" said Frank.

There was a slight pause, then Mr. Hardy continued earnestly. "Now here's the crux of the matter. That phone call was traced to Bayport."

"What?" Joe exclaimed.

"Yes. To be precise, from a phone booth in the north quadrant of the fairgrounds. I want you boys to stake out the place."

"That's going to be a little rough," Frank said. "Solo's Super Carnival came to town yesterday and set up at the fairgrounds. They're opening tonight. No telling how many people have used that particular phone."

"Oh? I see," Mr. Hardy said. "Perhaps the man we want is connected with the carnival."

Frank and Joe tingled with excitement. They had often helped their father on important cases and had gained some renown with their clever solutions.

The Tower Treasure was their first successful case, and not long ago they had solved the mystery of *The Secret Agent on Flight 101.*

"Dad, we'll go to the fairgrounds right away," Joe said.

"But wait. I have a word of advice," Mr. Hardy said seriously. "This may be a dangerous gang with a lot at stake. Take no unnecessary chances."

"We'll watch ourselves," Frank assured his father and they hung up.

Joe came downstairs to join his brother in studying their notes. They were still discussing the mystery half an hour later, when the doorbell rang. Frank rose, but Mrs. Hardy passed the living-room entrance on the way to the front door and motioned for him to sit down.

The boys heard the voice of a man and the name *Solo* and were out of their chairs in an instant and on the way into the foyer. Solo was a tall man with ruddy cheeks and good-humored eyes.

After Mrs. Hardy introduced her sons, Sid Solo said, "I sure am sorry Mr. Hardy's out of town. We've been plagued with pickpockets in the last six towns we've played. Bad for business, keeps the customers away. I thought if I hired Mr. Hardy—well, what with his reputation and all—those pickpockets would skedaddle pretty quick."

Frank winked at Joe, then said, "Mr. Solo, perhaps my brother and I can help you."

The carnival man beamed. "Why, I'd consider that a personal favor. I've heard of some of your exploits and I'll lay two-to-one odds that those cheap crooks won't be any happier with Fenton Hardy's sons on the job than they would be with your dad."

Solo hired the boys on the spot, told them he opened daily at three in the afternoon, and then left.

As soon as they had finished supper, Frank and Joe hurried out to their convertible and were on their way to Solo's Super Carnival. Frank was at the wheel.

"It's perfect," he said as they sped down the highway. "We can kill two birds with one stone—get rid of Mr. Solo's pickpockets and search for our mystery informer at the same time."

At the fairgrounds they parked in one of the spacious lots, with scores of other cars. As they walked toward the carnival, the voices of pitchmen could be heard shouting above the noise of a merry-go-round calliope. Delighted shrieks from riders on the roller coaster added to the buoyant feeling of the carnival. Frank and Joe strode briskly to one of the side gates, where there were not many patrons.

The ticket taker was a large, burly youth only a few years older than the Hardys.

Frank smiled. "We're the Hardys. Mr. Solo is expecting us."

Joe took a step toward the entrance, but the sullen-faced attendant blocked the way. "You're the Hardys! So what? You gotta buy a ticket!"

Frank explained their mission as sleuths, but the fellow kept shaking his head. "Get lost!"

Frank grew impatient. "I'll leave my brother here," he said. "But I'm going to find Mr. Solo,

bring him back, and get things straightened out."
He started past the booth.

The big ticket taker grabbed Frank roughly around the neck and threw him to the ground. Then he poised for a kick.

"Watch it, Frank!" Joe yelled and tackled the bully, bringing him to the ground with a thud.

With a curse, the ticket taker lunged to his feet and rained hammerlike blows upon Joe. At the same time, he threw back his head and bellowed, "Hey Rube!"

The traditional carnival trouble call sounded over the fairgrounds.

"Hey Rube!" he shouted again.

CHAPTER II

Whale of a Discovery

JOE's assailant paused only a split second, but it was time enough for the Hardy boy to land a roundhouse blow to the solar plexus of his opponent. The burly youth dropped face first, just at the moment when angry shouts filled the air. Joe glanced around to see a group of tough-looking roustabouts bearing down on them.

"Oh, oh, Frank. Here comes trouble."

"We'll try to talk our way out," his brother replied.

"There they are!" cried the leader of the carnival laborers. "They kayoed Knocker Felsen. Let's get 'em, boys!"

Frank and Joe stood shoulder to shoulder, braced to meet the charge. "Wait a minute!" Frank yelled.

"They're not going to listen," Joe said. "We're in for it now."

The carnival men had almost reached the boys, fists poised and eyes flashing, when an authoritative voice shouted, "Hold it! I'm Police Chief Collig, and I'll arrest the first one who throws a punch!"

The carnies hesitated and looked at one another uncertainly. Then, realizing that the chief's threat was not an idle one, they unclenched their fists and began to mill about. The men muttered angrily among themselves and cast sour glances at Frank and Joe.

"Wow!" said Joe when the police chief appeared at their side. "Are we glad to see you!"

"I can understand that," Chief Collig said. "It's a rough bunch. I'd like to know what's going on here."

Frank and Joe told him. By the time they finished their story, Knocker Felsen had regained his feet. Chief Collig vouched for the Hardys, but the carny leader was hard to convince. He looked dubiously at Frank and Joe.

"Well, if Mr. Solo hired them," he said finally, "and if you say they really are detectives, then I guess it's all right." He looked embarrassed. "Sorry about the trouble, fellows."

Frank and Joe accepted his apology. Knocker Felsen, however, with one hand pressed to the pit of his stomach, sulked away a few steps, grumbling.

"Let's shake and forget it," Frank said, but

Knocker refused the offer and marched back to his ticket booth.

"He's a real sorehead," Joe observed.

Chief Collig nodded. "I'd be a little careful of him."

The Hardys thanked the officer and wandered into the already crowded avenues of the carnival to begin their double duties. Near the merry-go-round Joe spotted a familiar figure.

"Hey, Chet!" he called.

Their best friend swiveled his ample frame around and trotted over to their side. His round, freckled face was attentive as Frank and Joe told him about the call from their father and about Sid Solo.

"How would you like to give us a hand, Chet?" Frank asked.

Chet Morton considered the offer silently. The husky boy was fond of fun and strongly opposed to hard work. He had no great taste for danger and usually backed away from it. But when Frank and Joe were in a tight spot, Chet always pitched in to help.

Finally he replied with a big smile, "Sure. This is the kind of detective work I like—observation and investigation. Everything from a distance."

The three laughed and sauntered down the carnival's midway, their eyes searching for suspicious characters. As they walked, Chet told them of his latest hobby—scrimshaw. He was constantly discovering new hobbies and sports, plunging enthusiastically into each one. But after a few weeks, his interest would wane.

Now it was scrimshaw—the art of polishing whale teeth and walrus tusks, then carving a picture or a design into the ivory. Frank and Joe were somewhat familiar with this art. They owned a walrus-tusk cribbage board, decorated by an Alaskan Eskimo.

"Scrimshaw really is the greatest," Chet bubbled. "Why, did you know that old-time sailors would spend as long as six months carving one single sperm whale tooth? And it's no wonder! Those fellows spent an average of three years on each whaling trip."

Chet explained how the ivory was softened by a soaking in brine, how its roughness was removed with a rasp, and later how it was polished with pumice and finally rubbed to a gloss with the palm of the hand.

"But, Chet," said Frank, "are you sure you have the patience?"

His friend was not listening. "The carving itself," he went on, "was done with sail needles or jackknives. Once the design had been etched on, they used India ink to stain the lines. Of course today some people use power tools, but that's not for me. No sir! I'll do it by hand."

"We've got a new hobby, too," Joe said. "Collecting lost relatives."

"What do you mean?" Chet asked, stopping beneath the platform on which Boko the Clown was doing a unicycle routine.

"Look at this!" Joe showed him the picture of Elmer Hardy and told of the impending visit. Chet chuckled over Elmer's picture and expressed the hope that the old seaman could teach him a few more things about scrimshaw.

Suddenly a hoarse cough sounded above the boys' heads. They looked up to Boko peering down at the photograph of Elmer Hardy.

"Excuse me, fellows," Boko said. "I just finished my act and I'm on my way off the platform."

The boys stepped aside. Boko leaped to the ground and disappeared around the corner of the canvas facade.

"I think," Frank said, "that this would be as good a time as any to start asking some questions."

Joe and Chet agreed, and Frank led the way around the corner in the direction Boko had taken. They found the clown drinking coffee in a small private resting place for the performers. He had taken off his dunce cap, but was still wearing his baggy polka-dot suit, his floppy shoes, and his red-and-white grease paint.

With him was Rembrandt the Tattooed Man. Rembrandt, wearing only bathing trunks, was covered from head to foot with multicolored tattoos of every imaginable kind. Included was a scene depicting whalers closing in on a huge sperm whale whose giant, blunt head rose far above the waves. This artistic gem covered Rembrandt's entire chest.

The boys introduced themselves. Rembrandt and Boko were friendly enough until Frank deftly turned the conversation to a criminal named Blackright and an unknown man who wanted to sell information about Blackright. Then Boko and Rembrandt grew distant. Their answers became curt.

Finally Boko said, "Look, you guys. We never heard of nobody named Blackright. We don't know nothin' about it. Now, why don't you leave us alone so we can take it easy a while? We got to go back on stage in a few minutes."

On the midway again, Joe shook his head. "It's possible," he said, "that they're telling the truth."

Frank looked dubious. "Carnival performers work hard and they need their coffee breaks," he said. "But their change of attitude was a bit too sudden for my taste."

Chet agreed with Frank, and the boys decided that Boko and Rembrandt definitely warranted further attention. Earlier, Chet had promised to meet his sister Iola and her friend Callie at the Venus Rocket Express. That was fine with the Hardys. Joe regarded vivacious, dark-haired Iola Morton as his regular date. Slender, blond, lithesome Callie Shaw was Frank's favorite partner.

"Hi, Joe!" Iola cried gaily when the boys

reached the roller coaster. "Are you and Frank going to take us up?" She cast a sidelong glance at her brother. "Chet wasn't at all happy with the idea."

"Aw, lay off!" Chet replied. "You know what that does to my stomach."

It was agreed that Frank and Joe would take the girls on the ride and that Chet would maintain the lookout for pickpockets while they were gone. The two couples hurried to the ticket booth, climbed into a red-and-green car, and started up a long incline. There was a breathless moment's hesitation at the peak; then a dizzying plunge down the steep drop that made the girls scream as the wind whipped their hair about. Iola and Callie clutched Frank and Joe for protection and hung on tightly until the coaster came to a stop.

The four young people emerged with bright eyes and happy expressions.

"Oh, oh," Frank said. "Look over by the shooting gallery, just behind Chet."

Their buddy was shadowing a seedy-looking man, watching his every move. Behind the stout sleuth was a clean-cut fellow in slacks and a sports jacket, whose appearance would have aroused no one's suspicion. As they watched, however, this man's hand removed a wallet from the back pocket of a short, balding onlooker beside him. The victim felt the touch and whirled around.

Panicky, the thief slipped the stolen wallet into Chet's pocket!

"Let's go!" Frank said. He and Joe rushed to the scene. The irate patron had seized the pickpocket, who in turn had denied his guilt and accused Chet. Poor Chet was bewildered and confused, especially when a quick search revealed the missing wallet in his possession.

"But listen," he said, befuddled, "I—I—" A crowd formed and the pickpocket tried to slip away. Frank and Joe grabbed him.

"All right, folks," Frank said. "Please go about your business. We're security detectives for Mr. Solo."

The pickpocket protested his innocence and said that "the fat kid" had stolen the wallet.

"For your information," Frank told him, "not only is Chet Morton a good friend of ours, but he's our assistant!"

Frank and Joe each took one of the pickpocket's arms and they escorted him with firmness to Sid Solo's private office. The victim came along to make the identification. Police Chief Collig was called, and after he had heard the story, one of his patrolmen ran the pickpocket out of town with a warning that if he showed up again he would be put behind bars.

Solo walked Frank and Joe back to the spot where they had left Chet with Callie and Iola.

The carnival man was in high spirits and heaped praise and congratulations upon the Hardys.

"I knew I'd get results with you two on the job," he said, clapping them on the shoulders.

Knocker Felsen was standing nearby. Upon hearing the praise he sneered, turned his back, and walked away to show his contempt.

The rest of the evening passed uneventfully. When the crowds thinned out and the carnival began to shut down, the Hardys said good night to Chet.

"So long, fellows," he replied. "I'm going to stash away a couple of pizzas Mr. Solo promised me."

Frank and Joe drove Callie and Iola home, then returned to their own house. Their mother was waiting for them with a twinkle in her eyes and a clipping from the evening newspaper in her hand.

"What have you got there, Mom?" Joe asked the slender, pretty woman.

"I think you might call it a whale of a story," Mrs. Hardy replied brightly. "Look!"

Her sons studied the clipping together. It read:

Earth-moving machines working at the site of the new Bayport shopping center this morning dug up a stuffed Blue Whale. The Blue Whale, largest of all sea-dwelling mammals, grows to nearly one hundred feet long. The Bayport whale is not that big, however. It had evidently been buried a long time.

"I'm all for digging up buried treasure," Joe said. "Matter of fact, we have several times. But old whales, no sir!"

"How do you suppose a whale ever got to Bayport?" Mrs. Hardy asked.

"Maybe during the ice age," replied Frank.

"But it was stuffed," his mother said.

"From overeating," Joe jested. Suddenly he exclaimed, "Hey! Mr. Prito has the contract for the shopping-center project, doesn't he?"

"He sure does," Frank said with a yawn. "Let's give Tony a call in the morning and ask him how it feels to be captain of the good whaling ship *Bulldozer*."

The next day after breakfast Frank was dialing Tony's number when the doorbell rang. Joe hastened through the living room to answer it.

"Frank," he called from the hall, "hang up. Tony and Biff are here."

The Hardys' school friends walked in, grinning. Tony Prito, a good-looking youth with black wavy hair and olive skin, was followed by Biff Hooper. Biff was tall, broad-shouldered, and the most rugged lineman on the Bayport High football team, of which Frank and Joe were star performers.

Tony raised his hands, signifying silence, before either Joe or Frank could get a word out. He took the pose of an orator.

"My friends," he said somberly, "you are looking at two very high-class entrepreneurs." He pointed to Biff, then to himself. "We have just purchased one legitimate whale—for a very fair sum, I might add—and we are going to show it to the good citizens of Bayport for fifty cents a look."

Tony jumped into the air and clicked his heels. "Yahoo! We're in business!" he exulted.

CHAPTER III

A Staunch Refusal

TONY stopped cavorting and talked seriously. "We bought the whale from the man who owns the property. He said there was nothing in the world he could do with a whale, and so he gave us a good price."

Biff chimed in, "The old blimp's in swell condition. It was protected with oilskins. We put in a good day's work scrubbing it down. Looks as good as new now."

"My father's letting us use that vacant lot he owns with a work shack on it," Tony said. "We spent all last evening putting up a big tarpaulin around our pet. Built a ticket booth, too."

He looked ruefully at the blisters on his hand. "We thought you Hardys might give us a hand and that all four of us could go into this thing together—be partners and share the profits."

"We'd like to, Tony," Frank said with a tinge

of regret. "It sounds like a lot of fun. But we have a couple of jobs to do. We're trying to find someone who's connected with a case Dad's working on, and at the same time we've been hired by Sid Solo to spot pickpockets at the carnival."

Tony was disappointed. "Well, maybe later. We'd sure like to have you with us."

Biff glanced at his watch. "Come on, Tony. We have a long day ahead of us."

As they moved toward the door, Aunt Gertrude entered the room. "Wouldn't you know it?" she said. "Every time I take a tray of fresh-baked cookies from the oven, our boys' friends show up!"

Biff grinned. "I see your aunt was up before breakfast." He turned to Tony. "On second thought, partner, it's not *that* late."

The boys followed Aunt Gertrude into the kitchen. "Where's Chet Morton?" she inquired. "He usually leads the charge when there's something edible around."

"The last time we saw him," Joe said, "he was polishing off pizzas at the carnival."

Aunt Gertrude stood proudly by while the boys finished their snack. Then Biff and Tony left, amid best wishes from their pals.

That afternoon Frank and Joe arrived at the carnival to find Sid Solo pacing around, very much upset. "Just look around you," he said with a wave of his hand.

The Hardys had been walking through the

grounds of Solo's Super Carnival for nearly an hour, and were well aware of the problem. The midways had been overflowing with patrons the night before. Wave after wave of them had surged from tent to tent—from side show to side show. But today there was only a trickle of customers. The few who had come were wandering aimlessly about, looking bored and spending little money.

"I don't understand it," Frank said. "Last night you'd have had a hard time keeping 'em away with artillery."

"It's those two fellows—Tony Prito and Biff Hooper!" Solo fumed.

"What have they to do with it?" Joe asked.

"It's that stupid whale of theirs. People figure they can always see a carnival, but a whale's a once in a lifetime thing. Prito and Hooper are stealing all my customers!"

Solo smacked a fist into his hand. "Well, I'm not going to sit around and watch my show go bankrupt. Come on! We're going to pay a call on those guys. I'll buy their silly whale, and that'll be the end of that!"

As they walked to Solo's station wagon, Frank and Joe explained that Biff and Tony were their friends, and really had not intended to take any business away from the carnival.

Grim-faced, Solo did not reply. He beckoned to Knocker Felsen, who was lounging in the shade of a tent, chewing on a long stalk of grass.

"Come along, Knocker!" Solo ordered. Felsen, looking pleased at the prospect of trouble, jumped into the front seat with Solo. The ride was short, and when they approached the lot on which the whale was located, a long queue was waiting to buy tickets.

Biff and Tony were in the shack which they were using as an office. They stepped out to greet the Hardys and the carnival duo.

Solo made his offer. Biff and Tony talked quietly for a moment, then Tony said:

"I'm sorry, Mr. Solo, but we can make more money by showing the whale ourselves."

"You're ruining me!" Solo cried.

"Mr. Solo," Biff said, "in a day or two, most of the people in Bayport will have seen our whale and they'll go swarming right back to your show."

"Maybe," the carnival owner replied. "But I can't afford three days like this."

Frank took Joe off to the side and whispered, "We're in a bad position. If we side with Mr. Solo, Biff and Tony will be angry. If we side against the carnival, then Mr. Solo will blow up. I have a plan that might make everybody happy. Back me up, okay?"

Joe nodded.

"Excuse me," Frank said. The argument between Solo, Biff, and Tony quieted. "Mr. Solo, why don't you pay Biff and Tony half of your original offer, take the whale and show it in your carnival, but pay a percentage to Biff and Tony on each ticket sold? That way people will come to the carnival, but the boys will still be making money."

"That sounds great," Joe said.

Solo scratched his head. "I don't know . . ."

"Don't do it, boss," Felsen urged. "Don't let these jerks hold you up."

Biff's temper flared. "Nuts to you. We'll keep the whale!"

Felsen bunched his big knuckles and lumbered forward. "You punk!" He flailed at Biff, landing a couple of clumsy but hard-hitting punches.

Biff quickly dropped into a boxer's defense position. Spotting an opening, he shot out his right fist. It hit Felsen squarely on the jaw. Glassy-eyed, he stumbled back and fell to the ground. Frank and Joe pinned him down before he could rise and attack again.

"Knocker!" Solo roared. "How many times have I told you not to go off half-cocked like that? You've ruined any chance we had of making a deal." He reached down, grabbed the big youth by the arm, and yanked him to his feet.

The telephone rang in the shack. Tony answered it while Biff kept a wary eye on Felsen. "Frank, Joe," Tony said. "It's for either one of you."

Joe took the call and spoke low, so as not to be overheard. Outside, Frank tried to smooth things over. Tony went so far as to tell Solo that he and Biff would think about his offer and that maybe they could discuss it again in a couple of days.

Solo and Felsen left, Knocker glowering over his shoulder at the boys. Solo said he would wait in the station wagon until Frank and Joe were ready to return to the carnival.

Joe finished his conversation and hung up. "It was Dad," he told Frank. Their father had first phoned home. Mrs. Hardy had directed him to call the carnival, where an aide to Solo had told him where his boss and the Hardys had gone.

"The informer called again last night," Joe went on, "and from the same booth! The police still won't pay the price he's asking for the information, but Mr. Dudley-Harris will, through Dad. We have to find out who made those calls, and soon!"

The young sleuths told Biff and Tony they were sorry for the trouble that had erupted. Their friends agreed it certainly was not the Hardys' fault. Sid Solo drove back to the carnival in silence, with Knocker Felsen brooding in the front seat and gingerly massaging his bruised jaw.

Back at the fairgrounds, there was not much for the Hardys to do, since pickpockets work only in crowds. The informer had never called during the day, and Frank decided that there was no reason for him to change his pattern. They worked out a plan whereby, as soon as darkness fell, one of them would maintain a vigil over the phone booth from a position of concealment within a carnival truck parked nearby.

They spelled each other, Frank taking a one-hour shift while Joe wandered through the carnival, and then reversing their roles for the next hour. It was nearly closing time and they had spotted nothing.

Frank was dejected. Maybe the informer had been frightened away! His spirits brightened considerably, however, when Joe came rushing up.

His brother had two facts to report. First, a slightly built youth with sandy hair had lurked in the shadows for more than half an hour near the telephone booth. He finally left. Five minutes later Boko the Clown appeared, entered the booth, and made a call. Joe had not been able to hear much of the conversation, but he did know that Boko had been arguing with someone about money!

"Let's go," Frank said. "It's time to ask Boko a few pointed questions."

They found the clown in his dressing room, still wearing his costume and makeup. At first he was angry and told the boys it was none of their business. But when Frank sternly reminded him of the seriousness of the case and of the severe punishment that would be meted out to the guilty parties, Boko changed his attitude.

"Look, fellows," he said plaintively. "I don't

know anything about any ivory statue or some joker named Blackright. I got angry, 'cause—well, it's a personal matter. I was arguin' with my wife about some bills." The clown looked down at his feet. "That's not the kind of thing you like to tell other people."

Frank and Joe told Boko they were sorry to have bothered him, and left. No further leads developed the remainder of the night. When the carnival closed, the Hardys went to Sid Solo's office. The owner was gloomily going over the figures of the day's gate receipts. Frank and Joe sat in chairs, relaxing.

"I was so sure he was our man," Joe said unhappily.

"Mr. Solo," said Frank, "does Boko argue with his wife about money very often?"

Without looking up, Solo said, "Boko? Ha, how could he? He's never been married."

"What!" the boys exclaimed in unison. They sprang to their feet and were out of the door in an instant, leaving Solo looking perplexed.

"Something fishy going on here," Frank stated, pausing to look around.

"I'll say!" Joe agreed. "This could be a big break in the case, Frank."

The Hardys separated, deciding they would have a better chance of finding Boko that way, and agreed to meet back at Solo's office in half an hour.

Frank questioned several carnival employees, but with no success. When the half hour was up he returned to Solo's office, hoping that Joe had had better luck.

Joe was not there. Fifteen minutes passed, then another fifteen. Frank grew nervous.

An hour after the appointed time Frank was forced to admit a disturbing fact—Joe had disappeared!

CHAPTER IV

Wheel of Danger

FRANK searched through the carnival frantically, his emotions in turmoil. If anything had happened to Joe . . . He set his jaw grimly and went on.

Sid Solo had enlisted half a dozen of his men to help Frank. They spread out through all parts of the darkened carnival, calling Joe's name, probing into pitch-dark tents and under trucks and wagons with flashlights.

None of the people Frank questioned had seen Joe. Nor, for that matter, had anyone seen Boko the Clown.

Frank stopped to catch his breath and leaned against the side of a booth. His anger and frustration had knotted the muscles in his shoulders. He forced himself to relax, knowing that a man who loses control of his emotions weakens his own cause.

There was a long, low-pitched creaking sound above him. Frank looked up and saw that the carnival's giant Ferris wheel was moving—ever so slightly. Then his eyes widened and his mouth dropped open with shock.

In the pale light of the full moon he could see a figure standing high above the ground in the uppermost car. It was Joe! He was blindfolded and his hands were tied behind his back. He was trying to feel his way out of the car.

"Joe! Sit down!" Frank screamed. "You're on top of the Ferris wheel. Don't try to get out or you'll be killed!"

Joe heeded his brother's warning and Frank sighed with relief.

"Frank!" Solo called from the distance. "Is that you? Have you found Joe?"

"We're at the Ferris wheel, Mr. Solo," Frank answered. "Come quick! We need you."

A few moments later Sid Solo burst upon the scene. "What's wrong, Frank?" he queried anxiously.

"Up there. Somebody bound and blindfolded Joe and put him on the wheel."

"Oh, no!" Solo said, horrified. He cupped his hands to his mouth and called up to Joe. "Sit tight, son. I'll have you down safely in just a minute."

He opened the plate covering the engine controls at the base of the Ferris wheel and fired the gas engine. Then he grasped the upright stick that dictated the motion of the wheel and gently eased it forward. Moments later Joe's car reached the ground. Frank pulled the blindfold from his brother's eyes and cut the bonds on his wrists with a penknife.

"Thanks," Joe said gratefully. "That was a close one."

"What happened?" Frank asked. "How did you get up there?"

Joe touched the back of his head and winced as his fingers made contact with the large bump. "I don't know. I was looking for Boko. I passed by the Ferris wheel, called his name, then someone clobbered me. When I came to, I stood up and that's when I heard your shout."

"Someone's going to pay for this," Frank vowed through clenched teeth.

"I hate to think that it was one of my people," Solo said, "but I did see someone slinking away as I came running."

"Who?" Frank demanded.

"I'm not sure. It was too dark for a positive identification, but it might have been Rembrandt."

"I'd like to talk to him," Frank said. "Along with Boko and Knocker Felsen."

"That goes double for me," Joe added.

A short time later the trio confronted Rembrandt, Felsen, and Boko in Solo's office. All the suspects firmly denied guilt.

"Let's get this straight," Frank said. "Boko, you

say that you were out taking a walk alone. Is that right?"

"Yeah."

"Well, if it was just a harmless walk," Frank continued, "then why did it come right on the heels of the lie you told us about your 'wife'?"

"That's my business," the clown snarled. "Money matters are personal. I don't have to tell anybody about them."

"What about you, Felsen?" Joe asked.

"I ain't gonna account to no punks for my actions," the big carny said.

"You'd better!" Solo snapped.

Felsen looked from his employer to the Hardys, then shrugged. "I was checkin' the animals—all alone."

"That leaves you, Rembrandt," Frank said.

"I was sound asleep in my wagon."

Frank pointed out that there was not a single witness who could back up any of their stories. He added that it looked very odd, but he admitted that since he and Joe had no proof, they had no choice but to drop the matter, at least for the present.

After a good night's sleep Joe was in fine shape. The lump on his head had gone down and his headache disappeared. The boys reported to the carnival in the afternoon and found about as much happiness as a ball team on the short end of a 50–0 score.

"We've had less than a hundred and fifty customers in the last day and a half," Solo told them. "I'm unable to meet my pay roll in full." Solo had arranged to close the carnival for an hour. He had called a meeting of all his employees, and invited Frank and Joe to attend.

The carnival people gathered under the roof of the largest tent on the lot. Some of them sprawled on the floor, others took up casual positions in the seats normally used by patrons. Everyone was glum. Solo mounted a platform and outlined the situation to them. When he explained that he could not pay full salaries that week, a loud grumbling broke out.

"Please," he said, "bear with me. We've been through hard times together before. We've survived, and we'll survive this time, too. As soon as business improves, I'll not only make up the back pay I owe, but give a bonus to every person here."

This promise seemed to help, but it was obvious that the carnival people were still not happy about the situation. Rembrandt rose to his feet. His face was hard.

"Boss, we got one big problem—the whale, right?"

Solo nodded.

"Well, I know a way to fix that," Rembrandt said. "And I sure ain't gonna waste no time doin' it."

"Wait a minute," Solo said. "It's true that the

sooner we can do something about the whale, the faster we'll climb out of the hole. But I want to make two things clear. One, there is to be *no* rough stuff, and two, I don't want anything dishonest done."

Rembrandt said nothing, just smiled.

After attending to a few more details, Solo ended the meeting.

"Some of these people are in pretty ugly moods," Frank said. "I think we'd better give Biff and Tony a call and tell them to keep a weather eye peeled for signs of trouble."

Before the young detectives had a chance to get to a phone, Boko the Clown came up behind them and placed a nervous hand on Joe's shoulder. Even the grease paint could not conceal the lines of tension around his mouth.

"Can I talk to you guys?" he asked, and glanced around furtively. "Some place where nobody can hear us."

"Sure," Frank said. The three of them went to a spot near the water-boat ride. "What is it?" Frank asked.

Boko's eyes flitted about. He said nothing until he was sure he could not be overheard. Then, in a frightened voice, he whispered, "They're out to get me. And if they do, I'm a dead man!"

Frank and Joe exchanged significant glances. "Who's out to get you?" Joe asked quickly.

"I can't tell you!" Boko said, trembling.

In his fear, the clown made a tight fist of his right hand. Frank's sharp eyes spotted a very curious tattoo. There were three blue marks on Boko's hand, one at the base of the thumb, one at the tip of the index finger, and the third at the base of the index finger. When Boko clenched his fist, these three portions joined to make a complete tattoo of a small whale. Frank made a mental note of this oddity.

The Hardys tried hard to persuade Boko to tell them more, but he refused. To their surprise, he took a thin, silver chain from around his neck and handed it to Frank. A small key was attached to the chain.

"If anything happens to me," Boko said, "I want you to go to my bunk wagon. Turn up the mattress and you'll find a loose board. There's a strongbox under the board. Open it up, and you'll know what to do."

A small group of concessionaires walked toward the trio. Boko saw them coming and he scampered away.

"We're on to something all right," Frank said. "Let's give Boko the night to calm down, then maybe he'll answer some questions for us tomorrow."

As the Hardys drove home, lightning pierced the night sky. They were scarcely in their bedroom when a fierce thunderstorm drenched the Bayport area.

Next morning they were eating Aunt Gertrude's hearty breakfast of eggs, sausages, wheatcakes and blueberry muffins and watching the early-morning newscast on television when the announcer said:

"Bayport police have a king-sized mystery to contend with this morning. Sometime during the night the Blue Whale belonging to Tony Prito and Biff Hooper was stolen. Tony Prito, who was standing guard, is missing and . . ."

Frank and Joe did not wait to hear any more. They delayed only long enough to tell their mother and Aunt Gertrude what had happened, then dashed out to their car. Moments later they were speeding to Tony's house. When the Hardys reached there, Police Chief Collig's car was just pulling up to the curb. Tony was in Collig's car, his clothes dirty and torn, his expression glazed.

Mr. Prito, a sturdy-looking man, dashed down the front steps and ran to his son. When Tony was settled comfortably in a chair in the living room, he told his story. Someone had slashed the tarpaulin with a knife and tried to get at the whale. Tony drove him off, but did not get much of a look at the intruder. Taking no chances, Tony decided to stand guard all night. The last thing he remembered was smelling something strange. Then he fell into unconsciousness.

"Gas!" Joe said.

Police Chief Collig nodded agreement. Tony

had awakened less than an hour before, near the entrance to the carnival.

"Those people are responsible!" Mr. Prito stormed. "They should be prosecuted!"

Chief Collig pointed out that no matter what they suspected, they had no proof. Tony's father reluctantly had to admit this was true. Mrs. Prito, still shaken by the night-long vigil waiting news of Tony, fussed like a mother hen over her son.

"I'm okay," Tony insisted. "Forget about me. There's only one thing I want." He turned to Chief Collig and the Hardys. "Find that whale!"

CHAPTER V

How Was It Done?

WHEN the Pritos' family doctor assured them that Tony would be all right after a day's rest, Frank and Joe drove to the site of the whale heist. But after a careful search, they had turned up no clues to the thieves.

"We can't even locate any truck tracks," Joe said ruefully. "The rain washed out everything."

"Maybe it wasn't carried off by a truck," Frank said thoughtfully.

"How else, then?" Joe retorted impatiently. "They sure didn't carry it off on their shoulders."

"I don't know, Joe. It just doesn't make any sense to me. We'll have to dope this out later."

Deciding that a further examination of the site would be fruitless, the Hardys returned to Tony's house. Now that Tony was over the initial shock of his experience he might be able to tell them something he hadn't remembered before.

"I'm sorry, fellows," Tony said apologetically, "but everything's a blank from the moment I got a whiff of that gas until the moment I woke up."

Biff Hooper, who had rushed to the Prito house as soon as he had learned the news, was stalking up and down the living room.

"Boy!" he said angrily. "Would I like to get my hands on Knocker Felsen. I'll bet anything he's the one who did this. I shouldn't have let him off so easy the first time!"

"Hold it," Frank said. "We can't leap to conclusions, Biff."

"Wait a sec!" Joe cried suddenly. "I know how they could have stolen the whale. A helicopter! A big cargo helicopter, powerful enough to hoist the whale up on cables and fly away with it!"

"Hey! That just might be it!" Frank agreed excitedly. "Let's phone Jack Wayne and see what he can tell us about helicopters in the area."

Jack was Fenton Hardy's personal pilot and a close friend of many years' standing. He told Frank and Joe he would get a rundown on all helicopters, including those for hire, within a fifty-mile radius of Bayport and call back. It did not take him long to gather the information.

"Frank, I hate to disappoint you," Jack reported, "but the storm last night was pretty widespread and there wasn't a single helicopter flying."

"I guess we can knock out that possibility," Frank said. "I still think Joe's idea is a good one, though. Somehow, I'm sure it was done by air. After all, even if you could find a truck big enough, you couldn't just drive through the middle of town with a whale!"

"Not without being noticed by an awful lot of people," Jack agreed.

"I think it would be worth our while to do some scouting by air. Would you get our plane ready right away, Jack?"

"Sure thing."

Forty-five minutes later the Hardys were at Bayport Airport. Both boys were licensed pilots. Frank slid behind the control wheel, obtained clearance from the tower, then taxied the single-engine, blue-and-white plane to the active runway and took off.

Frank flew around Bayport in ever-widening circles, drifting farther and farther from the city, while Joe scanned the ground through high-power binoculars. Four hours of searching were in vain.

"We're below the halfway mark," Frank said, indicating the gas gauge. "I think we should go down and refuel."

"Right," his brother answered. "Harrington Field is ten miles to the east. That's where they have the Strato Balloon Club. So keep an eye peeled."

Harrington Airport had a single paved runway pretty much off the mainstream of air traffic. It had only a rickety office building and one gas pit. Frank guided the plane down to a gentle landing, then taxied to the pit. Grizzled old Mr. Harrington came out to meet them.

"Hi, Frank. Hi, Joe. Top her off?"

"Okay," said Frank. While the man pumped gas into the plane, he added, "What's new, Mr. Harrington?"

"Only thing new around here," the man replied with a snort, "is that someone stole a couple of balloons belonging to the club. What do you think of that?"

"Pretty mean," Joe said. "We'll keep a lookout for the balloons."

The boys paid him for the gas and took off. Half an hour later Joe pointed to a stand of oak trees and cried, "Look there!"

Frank took the plane as low as he safely could and Joe got an excellent look through the binoculars. He relayed what he saw to Frank. "Those are the balloons all right. They're torn apart—all deflated. And, Frank, there are ropes attached to them, ropes with frayed ends!"

Satisfied, they headed back to Bayport. The method of the theft was now clear to them. The whale had been lifted silently and efficiently from its resting place by the balloons. The thieves evidently had depended upon air currents to carry it to whatever site they had selected. But the storm had wrecked their plans and the balloons as well.

Somewhere along the line the whale had been torn loose and lost.

As soon as they landed at Bayport Airport, Frank reported their find to Harrington. Then he called Jack Wayne and asked him to check on the wind velocity and direction over Bayport the previous night.

"Give us all the meteorological info you can get your hands on," Frank urged.

The boys had something to eat and then drove out to the carnival.

Now that the carnival had no competition, business was booming. Sid Solo was happy about this, but he was wringing his hands over a new problem.

"Boko's act is due to start in ten minutes," he said. "But he's disappeared. What am I going to do? The tent is packed and the customers are going to raise a big ruckus if I can't give them a clown."

"Boko's gone?" Frank exclaimed with alarm.

"Yes. He hasn't been seen since late last night."

Frank said to Joe, "I think we'd better call Chief Collig and tell him to be on the lookout. Boko's either in danger, as he told us last night, or else he's tied in with the stolen whale."

As Joe went to call Chief Collig, Solo moaned. "There's no way out of this one. Those people are going to want their money back, and I don't blame them."

"Cheer up, Mr. Solo," Frank said. "I think we can find a clown for you."

Solo's head snapped up. "Who? Where?"

"Chet's been on pickpocket duty until we got here, right?"

Solo nodded.

"Well, we're back," Frank said.

Afraid of being disappointed, Solo was almost unwilling to let himself hope. "Do you think Chet will . . . ?"

"We won't know until we ask him."

They found Chet and put the question to him. The chubby boy grinned and said, "Well, sounds like fun. Sure, I'd be happy to."

Solo pumped his hand. "Thank you. Thank you. If you pull this one off, you have my permission to eat free at every food concession in the carnival."

"Let's go!" Chet said eagerly.

The trio rushed to the costume and makeup trailer, hastily fitted Chet out in a clown suit, and daubed his face with grease paint. Solo grabbed a handful of props and stuffed them into Chet's pockets.

"It's time," Solo cried. He took Chet's hand and pulled the tubby youth toward the big tent. "Wait here until I call you."

A bareback riding troupe had just completed its act and the ringmaster was standing in the center of the arena looking unsure of himself. Apparently he did not know what announcement to make since the next slot was Boko's. Solo rushed forward, waved to the crowd, then took the microphone from the ringmaster.

"Ladies and gentlemen and children of all ages," he announced. "Due to circumstances beyond our control, Boko will not appear." The audience made loud sounds of disappointment. "But," Solo hurried on, "we have been very fortunate in securing for you the services of—of Chesterton the Great!" He turned away from the microphone and whispered to the bandleader, "Give 'em Number Three."

The band struck up a very serious and pompous march.

"Oh, oh," Chet said nervously. "That's for me."

"Good luck," Frank said.

Chet moved into the arena. He walked with great and exaggerated dignity, then suddenly he tripped and fell, shot quickly to his feet, and whirled around as if to see who had tripped him. The crowd roared at Chet's antics.

Chet shook his fist at them and stalked over to the nearest seats in mock anger. He selected a man and pointed a plastic flower at him, then showed the rest of the audience a squeeze bulb that would send water squirting into the man's face. He pressed the bulb—and the water squirted out the *back* of the flower into Chet's face! Chet feigned surprise and the audience howled with delight.

Next, the newly born clown drew a long chalk line on the floor. He opened a tiny umbrella, then stepped gingerly onto the chalk line, as if it were a wire stretched high above the ground, and began a balancing routine. The audience was laughing heartily by the time Solo rejoined Frank, who was howling in glee. Solo chuckled.

"It's really great!"

"I'd love to stay and watch," Frank said. "But I think there's something we should do." He told the carnival owner of Boko's instructions concerning the strongbox.

"Well," said Solo, "I think the situation justifies your opening it."

They left the Big Tent, found Joe, and went to Boko's wagon. As they drew near it, a figure burst from inside and dashed away.

"After him!" Joe shouted.

Frank threw all his strength into the chase, moved ahead of Joe and Solo, and gained on the fugitive. The man rounded a corner, Frank close behind. Then suddenly a low-strung tent rope caught Frank by the ankle and sent him pitching headlong to the ground. Joe and Mr. Solo came pounding up as Frank was pushing himself to his feet.

"What happened?" Joe asked.

"I tripped," Frank said disgustedly. "We'll never find him in the crowd now."

The crowd roared at Chet's antics

"Are you all right?" Joe asked.

"Fine. Let's get back to Boko's wagon and see what that guy was up to."

They walked back, mounted the wagon's steps, and pushed through the half-open door. "I smell smoke," Joe said.

Frank sniffed the air. "You're right."

The young detectives went directly to Boko's bunk, pulled up the mattress, and after a moment's search located the loose board. Frank raised it and stared into the empty hole. "The box is gone!"

A quick check of the wagon turned up the missing container under a pile of rags in a corner.

"I found it!" Joe exclaimed. Mournfully he added, "We're too late!"

He held the strongbox up for Frank and Solo to see. The lock had been broken open. The box was empty!

CHAPTER VI

A Well-Salted Guest

"WE missed it by minutes," Joe said. He set the strongbox down and shook his head. "Another blind alley."

"Let's search the wagon," Frank suggested. "The intruder might have left something behind that could prove valuable to us."

Frank, Joe, and Solo began a methodical investigation, opening storage lockers, tilting back the few pieces of furniture, running their fingers along cracks and crevices.

"Here's something!" Frank exclaimed suddenly. Solo and Joe gathered around him. On the floor near the entrance, mashed by a heel, was a small mound of dark, flaky ashes. "This accounts for the smoke you smelled, Joe. Whoever was in here must have burned the contents of the strongbox."

Frank sifted the ashes and snatched out a fragment of yellow paper that had not been consumed. "We're in luck!"

He held the brown-edged piece of paper up to the light. A few words were still legible: *Whitey Meldrum knows a . . .*

"Did you ever hear of a Whitey Meldrum?" Frank asked Solo.

"No. The name doesn't mean a thing to me."

Frank put the scrap of paper into his wallet. Further search revealed nothing. They left the wagon. As they were descending the three steps to the ground, Joe said, "Look!" He bent and retrieved a torn photograph. Its edge was charred and there was a smear of chewing gum on it.

"This must have been in the strongbox," Joe surmised. "The fire didn't get it and it probably stuck to the thief's foot when he ran out."

The picture was of a wiry man, hawk-faced, and dressed in circus tights. Solo identified him as an aerial artist named Kane who had been killed some years ago in a fall from a high wire.

"Well," Frank said, "we're on to something, but I'm not sure what. I think our next move should be to get in touch with Dad."

Joe agreed. They thanked Solo for his help, left the carnival, and drove home. There they related the day's events to their mother and aunt.

Mrs. Hardy said, "Your father would want to be brought up to date."

"He certainly would," Aunt Gertrude sputtered. "You should turn it all over to him. You boys have gone every bit as far as you should, maybe even farther. You're out of your depth, and it's too dangerous."

"Don't worry, Aunty," Joe said. "We're being careful."

The boys attempted to call their father at the New York hotel in which he was staying. The desk clerk told them Mr. Hardy was out; in fact, he had not been seen for the last forty-eight hours.

"That's odd," Frank said.

"He's probably tracking down a lead," Joe commented.

Frank suggested they try a radio message and the boys went up to their "ham" short-wave shack in the attic.

Their radio equipment was separate from that in their father's study. It included a receiver, a transceiver with VOX hookup, a signal generator, and a phone patch. Colorful QSL cards studded the wall over their gear, attesting to contacts with hams all over the world.

Time and again the boys called for their father to come in. No luck. Finally Frank clicked off the radio with a sigh and stood up.

"Dad must really have gone underground if he's not answering our radio call," Joe said as they trotted down the attic stairs.

"He probably has a hot lead," Frank said, "and doesn't want to risk breaking his cover."

When they reached the first floor they found Aunt Gertrude all atwitter. "Elmer Hardy called," she told them. "He's arriving at eight o'clock tomorrow morning!"

"That's great!" Joe said with a wide grin.

"But we didn't expect him that soon, and we'll have to prepare the guest room and . . ."

"Don't worry, Aunty. You'll have plenty of time in the morning. We'll pick him up and meanwhile you can straighten up the house."

The next morning the boys drove to the bus terminal, parked the car, then scanned the crowded waiting room. Elmer Hardy, looking like some romantic figure straight out of the Great Age of Exploration, was not difficult to spot. His sun-bronzed skin, great mane of hair, thick beard, and rough seaman's garb set him miles apart from the rest of the travelers.

"Cousin Elmer!" Frank called out. "Oh, Cousin Elmer!"

The man swiveled his head and his face lit up with pleasure. "You must be Frank and Joe," he said, hastening through the crowd toward them. His right arm was in a sling, so he used his left hand to shake hands. Then the visitor stood back and looked the youths over from head to foot.

"Well, knock me down with a belayin' pin! I can hardly believe that you are Fenton's sons. Why, you're practically full-growed!"

"We're really happy to meet you, Cousin Elmer.

From what Aunt Gertrude tells us, you're practically a family legend."

"Oh, pshaw! Just call me Elmer. Nothin' legendary about me. I'm an old sea dog, that's all."

"Did you break your arm?" Frank said solicitously.

"Nope. Just a strain. Got it heftin' my duffel bag the wrong way. Speakin' of that, hate to bother you, but could you boys give me a hand?"

"Glad to," Joe said.

Elmer walked to the baggage claim area and pointed out a huge canvas sea bag with his name stencilled upon it. "There she be."

"Wow!" Joe said. "I'll bet that took up half the bus."

Elmer laughed. "Only a quarter of it, boys, only a quarter."

Frank and Joe lugged Elmer's bag to the car, placed it in the rear seat, then drove their cousin home. Elmer greeted Laura Hardy and Aunt Gertrude with warmth, and as he kissed each of them fondly on the cheek, tears glistened in his eyes.

Aunt Gertrude had prepared a hearty breakfast and Elmer pitched into the food with great gusto. He was reluctant to talk about his past except in general terms.

"Oh, there were good times and bad times, just like in anybody's life, I guess." He sighed. "I'm well into middle age now and these last few years I really been hankerin' to see my relatives. Just think—me being cousin to the famous Fenton Hardy. I'm awfully sorry he's not here. But enough about me. Fill me in on what all of you have been doin' over the years."

Later Joe and Frank asked to be excused, since they wanted to see Tony.

They found he had made a fine recovery, and that the doctor had said it would be all right for him to get out of bed. Frank and Joe went down to the spacious recreation room, where Tony was pacing up and down.

"I don't care if Mr. Solo did call me and offered to help in any way he could," he fumed. "I say those carnival people did it!"

Biff Hooper, lounging on a couch, supported Tony. "I'm with you!"

"Even if it was someone from the carnival," Frank said, "I just don't think Mr. Solo was in on it. Sure, he's an excitable guy, and your whale exhibit was taking business away from the carnival but I feel he's okay."

"That may be," Biff said. "But I'm not so sure about that goon Felsen. And for that matter, Boko and Rembrandt don't seem to be Cub Scout leaders, either."

"Speculation's an integral part of detective work," Frank said. "But what we need now are facts. Facts!"

"Who's fat?" said a voice from the stairs. Then Chet clomped down into the recreation room.

"Fellows," Joe said with a sweep of his hand, "I give you Chesterton the Great!"

Biff and Tony applauded with the Hardys. Chet made a comic bow, then crossed the room and slumped wearily into an easy chair. "Oof! I just had a dozen pancakes for breakfast!" He patted his middle section and rolled his eyes.

Just then Mrs. Prito came down to the recreation room bearing two steaming hot mushroom and sausage pizzas. She smiled. "I thought I might interest someone in a snack," she said. "Any takers?"

"You bet!" said Biff. Tony opened some bottles of soda while Biff helped Mrs. Prito cut the pizza.

"Chet? How about you?" Mrs. Prito asked.

"Oh, I couldn't," he groaned. Then, a brief moment later, he said, "Well, just a little to keep up my strength." He helped himself to a large wedge.

The boys ate silently. Midway through a hot triangle of pizza, Frank looked up suddenly.

"I just remembered something about Boko," he said, and told the others about the clown's strange whale tattoo. "Think there might be any connection between that and the missing whale?"

Biff shrugged. "It's probably just coincidence."

"You know," said Joe, "Rembrandt has a whale tattooed on his chest. That makes three whales."

Tony looked doubtful. "Still coincidence. Tattooed men have all kinds of designs and pictures on their bodies. There's no reason why a whaling scene shouldn't be one of them."

"Still," Joe said, "three whales . . ."

"Four whales!" Chet cried, springing to his feet. The others stared at him.

"Frank," Chet said, "didn't you tell me that the name on the note sent to R. R. Dunn offering the Ivory Idol for sale was Blackright?"

"Yes," Frank answered. "What of it?"

"Well, Blackright is a whale, too!"

CHAPTER VII

Night Attack

"How do you know?" Frank asked in surprise.

"Scrimshaw's the answer to that," Chet replied proudly. "I've learned a lot in my hobby. It's pretty hard to study the art of carving whale ivory without picking up some information on whales themselves."

"That's obvious," Joe said. "Come on, Chet. Get to the point."

As the only person in the room who knew the answer to the riddle, Chet was enjoying his position and consequently in no hurry.

"Look," he said. "First, there are two general classes of whales: toothed whales, like the Sperm Whale and the Killer Whale and the Bottlenose and so on. And what they call baleen whales. None of the whales in this last group—the group, incidentally, that Tony and Biff's Blue Whale belonged to—have any teeth. They all have a series of 'plates' in their mouths that act like giant sieves. They swim around with their mouths open, take in a couple of tons of water that has food in it like shrimps and tiny fish, then close their mouths and expel the water through the plates, or as they're properly known—through the *baleen*."

"Listen, Chet," Frank put in quickly, "get us off the hook! Tell us about Blackright."

"That's what I'm doing," Chet protested.

"In the most roundabout way I've ever seen," Tony said with a long sigh.

"Ah," Chet went on, "to think of the tragedies that befall people such as I, who try to bring enlightenment to the world."

"Come on," Biff growled. "I can't take any more of this."

"Okay, okay," Chet resumed quickly. He explained that when men first started pursuing whales they called the most-sought-after variety Right Whales. One in this category was black, hence the name Blackright.

Chet wore a smug expression and folded his arms.

"Is that all?" Tony asked.

"*All!*" Chet said. "I think it's quite a bit!"

"It's an intriguing bit of deduction, Chet," Frank said. "We'll keep it in mind."

"Sounds pretty far-fetched to me," Tony remarked.

"I think the chain of whales is a good theory,"

Joe said, "but for the moment let's concentrate on what we *know* to be true."

Chet whacked his forehead with his palm.

"*Aiieee!* The trials and tribulations we geniuses go through."

"Fellows," Frank said, "duty calls. Let's drive to the carnival. Later, when the crowds are gone we could go to the spot where Tony regained consciousness and see if we can turn anything up."

All agreed. They left Tony's house, piled into the Hardys' convertible, and drove to the fairgrounds. After the carnival had shut down for the night, the four boys spread out so as to cover more ground, each probing with a flashlight beam as he searched for possible clues. Their efforts took them farther and farther away from each other, and so, thinking he was alone, Frank was startled when a hand dropped on his shoulder. He whirled around, ready to meet an attack.

"Frank, it's me!" came Joe's urgent whisper.

Frank relaxed. "You took me by surprise. What happened to your flashlight?"

"I doused it on purpose. I was scouting near the gate and caught sight of someone moving from shadow to shadow toward one of the carnival wagons—Knocker Felsen's, to be exact."

"We might lose him if we stop to get any of the other guys," Frank decided. "Better handle this one alone."

"That's why I came for you. Let's hurry."

Frank extinguished his own flashlight and the two made their way stealthily toward Knocker Felsen's wagon.

"There," Joe whispered. "See him?"

Frank squinted against the blackness and made out the dim silhouette of a crouched figure moving toward the wagon. "Let's not jump the gun. We'll wait until it's absolutely certain he's going to break into Felsen's quarters," Frank advised.

"Right."

They watched the figure advance a few more steps, pause, move forward and pause again.

"He's reached the steps," Joe said tensely. The intruder dashed up the steps and reached for the door. "Let's take him!" Frank yelled.

As the boys rushed forward, the figure poised before Felsen's door and spun to meet them. Frank was the first to get to the wagon and his speed earned him a punch in the jaw that sent him sprawling.

Joe came running and was hit like a tackling dummy. *Crash!* Both he and the stranger hit the ground. Frank shook his head to clear the cobwebs, sprinted to the struggling pair, and leaped into the fray. "Wow!" he thought. "This is one tough cookie!"

Their adversary fought with skill and power; only Frank's agility and quick reflexes saved him from being kayoed.

But suddenly he spotted an opening, seized his

opponent by the wrist, spun on his heel and threw him over his shoulder. The intruder hit the ground with a thud and Frank pinned him.

Voices sounded in the distance as Joe thumbed his flashlight to life. The Hardys gasped as the beam revealed the face of *Biff Hooper!*

At the same time, sleepy-eyed Knocker Felsen poked his head from the wagon with a blank look.

Biff groaned. He saw Frank and Joe, shook his head, and said, "Boy, you guys play awfully rough!"

"Us!" Frank fingered a bruise. "What about you?" In a lower voice he added, "What were you doing, sneaking up on Felsen like that?"

Frank had relaxed his grip and Biff got to his feet. "We all know he did it. I was going to force a confession out of him."

"Biff," Joe said, "that's no way to do detective work!"

"I guess so," Biff said dejectedly. "How come you jumped me?"

"We didn't know it was you," Frank answered. "How come *you* lit into us like that?"

Biff grinned. "Same reason you came after me—I didn't know who you were."

Flashlights bobbed toward the trio and a moment later Chet and Tony arrived. Close on their heels came Sid Solo.

"What's going on here?" he demanded.

"Yeah, what's up?" chimed in Knocker.

"Just a bit of a mix-up," Joe explained. "We came back in the hope of finding new clues and we—ah—stumbled over each other in the dark."

Felsen yawned, squinted against the bright lights, and lumbered back to bed.

Solo was sympathetic and again expressed regret over the theft of the whale.

"We just can't give up," Frank said. "Mr. Solo, would it be all right if we had another look around Boko's wagon?"

Solo consented. He went with them to the clown's quarters and opened the padlocked door with a key from his chain. Solo and the five youths gave the wagon a fine-toothed combing, but at the end of an hour they had found nothing of any value.

"It's hopeless," Joe said. "I think we'd better call it a night."

Biff finished thumbing through a file of magazines and tossed them on Boko's bunk. One slipped to the floor, and the corner of a postcard protruded from the pages. Frank's alert eyes caught sight of it.

"Hey, Biff, did you see that?" he exclaimed, pulling the card out.

"No. Must have missed it."

The others looked around him while he examined the card. It bore the postmark "Mystic, Conn." and the message *"Getting hot. Beluga."*

"Beluga!" Chet cried out. "I told you! Now will you believe me?"

"What do you mean?" Tony asked.

"Beluga's another name for the White Whale. Just try and tell me it's another coincidence!"

The boys now had to agree with Chet. This could no longer be chalked up to chance. Perhaps the whale names were the key to a code, Frank suggested.

During the ride back to Tony's house, they discussed the various developments in the mystery.

Frank and Joe dropped Biff off on the way, then left Tony at his home and said good night to Chet.

Their husky pal, beaming with success, got into his jalopy. Before he started the motor, Joe cautioned, "For Pete's sake, easy on the backfire, Chet. Everybody's asleep around here."

"Sure," came the answer, then *blam!* The chassis jiggled as the engine started, and Chet sheepishly headed for the farm where he lived, on the outskirts of Bayport.

Back at the Hardy house, Joe said, "Beluga, Blackright, Rembrandt's tattoo, Boko's tattoo and the missing whale! I just can't fit the pieces together."

"I can't either," Frank said. "But I think it might be worth while to make a trip to Mystic and—"

Frank was interrupted by a short ring of the

telephone. Aunt Gertrude called from the kitchen, "Boys, is Chet here?"

"No," replied Joe.

"Well, pick up the phone. Iola Morton's on."

Joe grabbed the extension phone in their father's study. "Hello, Iola. Isn't it rather late for a growing girl to be up?"

But his banter was short-lived. He sensed immediately that something was wrong.

"Joe," Iola said in a quavering voice, "I just talked to Tony. I'm worried. Chet should have been home long ago. We haven't seen or heard from him at all!"

CHAPTER VIII

A Fishy Cargo

"I'M sure Chet's all right, Iola," said Joe, trying to soothe the worried girl. "He probably had a flat tire, or just stopped for a late snack. Tell you what. Frank and I will go look for him, and as soon as we find him, we'll give you a call. Okay?"

"Thank you, Joe. I knew I could depend on you."

When Joe hung up and told Frank, the older boy looked concerned. "I don't like the sound of this. Chet could change a flat in ten minutes and be on his way again."

"I know," Joe said. "But there wasn't any sense in worrying Iola any further."

"Right." Frank reached in his pocket for his car keys. "We'd better get started."

Joe was just opening the front door when two muffled explosions split the still night air.

"Speak of the devil!" Frank exclaimed with obvious relief.

Chet's battered old jalopy pulled up to the curb. The car backfired a third time before sputtering into silence on the quiet street. Chet jumped out and ran up to Frank and Joe.

"Have I got something to tell you!" he blurted. "A fantastic piece of luck!"

"All right," Joe said, "but first you'd better call your sister. She's worried about you."

"Oh." An expression of regret crossed Chet's face. "I know I should have phoned, but I had to get here as fast as I could."

"Come on in," Frank said. "Call Iola and let her know where you are, then tell us about it."

Chet quickly telephoned his sister, then announced to the boys, "I've found another whale!"

"Where?" Joe asked. "What kind?"

"California Gray. When I left you guys I headed straight out of town on the parkway. You know Marty's Giant Burgers place?"

"Sure," Frank answered.

"Well, I was feeling a little hungry so I stopped in for a quick bite. There was a fellow sitting at the counter next to me—a big man, rough-looking, strong. His shirtsleeves were rolled up, and when he raised his coffee cup, I saw the tattoo. It was a small one on his right biceps. As good a picture of a California Gray as I've ever seen."

Chet said that when the man had noticed him staring at the tattoo, he had gulped down the remainder of his coffee, paid his bill quickly, and hastened out of the diner.

"I followed him," Chet said. "He got into the cab of a large tractor truck—a *very large* truck!"

"Large enough to hide a Blue Whale in?" Frank asked.

"I'm not sure," Chet said. "But I do know that it was one of the biggest trucks I've ever seen. And to top it off, it was a Connecticut license plate. I remembered the postcard clue, and here I am!"

"What are we waiting for?" Joe asked.

"Not a thing," Frank said, heading for the Hardys' car. "Did you get the license number, Chet?"

"You bet I did." Chet produced a scrap of paper on which he had written the plate number.

The boys sped down the highway, overtaking several trucks, but not the one they wanted. Joe had done some quick computations and reckoned they should close the remaining gap within the next half hour.

"There it is!" Chet cried finally.

The truck was a huge tractor-trailer combination with twin diesel exhaust stacks that belched thick, acrid columns of smoke into the air. Frank moved the car into a position that was a short, but safe distance behind the roaring behemoth.

"What do we do now?" Joe asked.

"I'll wait for an open stretch of road," Frank said. "Then I'll move into the next lane and pull abreast of the cab. When the driver can see you, motion for him to swing onto the shoulder and stop."

"What if he doesn't?" Joe queried.

"We'll assume he's got something to hide, and we'll find the nearest phone, call the State Police and have him stopped."

"That's a fine plan if it works," Chet said fearfully. "But what if he waits until we're alongside, then decides to run us off the road?"

"It's a risk we'll have to take," Frank answered coolly. "I'll be on my guard. Everyone set?"

The car swung into the passing lane and zipped forward.

"A little bit more, just a bit more," Joe said tensely. The two vehicles were almost nose and nose. Joe began waving for the truck driver to pull over. Nothing happened.

"He either doesn't understand, or he's just not going to stop," the boy shouted above the roar of the truck's motor.

"Looks as if we have our answer!" Frank bellowed. "I think it's time to call the police."

"Wait a minute!" Joe yelled. The truck's directional signal blinked like a big red eye as the thundering wheels eased onto the shoulder of the highway.

Frank pulled in behind on the gravel strip and stopped. The three boys leaped out and ran forward to where the truck had hissed to a halt. The driver climbed down from his cab to meet them. To the Hardys' surprise, he wore a friendly smile.

"What's the trouble, guys?" he asked. "Motor problems or something?"

The boys were taken aback by the trucker's unexpected good humor. Frank suddenly realized they might have made a mistake. "One question," he said. "What's the tattoo on your right arm?"

The boys were poised, ready to spring into action at the first sign of a hostile move.

The driver touched his arm. "You mean Hilda?" he asked, bewildered.

"Hilda?" Frank repeated with equal confusion.

"Sure." The truck driver exposed his arm and offered his tattoo for the youths' inspection. He even jiggled his biceps. "She's just something I had put on while I was in the U.S. Navy."

The boys gaped. The tattoo was a girl in a bikini reclining on one elbow.

"You and your California Gray Whale!" Joe exploded at Chet.

The stout boy stared at his feet with embarrassment. "Well, if you look at it from an angle, it does look like a Gray Whale. And besides, you Hardys are always drumming into my head that no possible clue can be overlooked."

"You do have a point there," Frank admitted.

"Hey, guys!" the trucker said. "Since you pulled me off the road, would you mind letting me in on the story?"

The boys apologized, then told the driver who they were and what they were doing. The man, who gave his name as Adam Snow, burst out laughing. "So you thought I might have a whale in here, eh?" He led them to the back of the truck and opened the massive doors. Instantly a pungent, fishy odor assailed the young sleuths' nostrils.

"Eight tons of salted fish," Snow said, pointing to the stacked barrels. "But it's all mackerel and herring, not whale!"

The boys chatted with Snow a while longer. Learning he had been raised in Mystic, they asked him if he could recommend a place to stay.

"That's easy," Snow told them. "Best place in town belongs to Mrs. Elmira Snow, my mother! She rents rooms, sets the finest table you can find, and her place is within walking distance of the Marine Historical Museum."

The boys thanked Snow and the four of them parted with a hearty round of handshakes. On the ride back home, Joe teased Chet again about his California Gray Whale.

"Look at it this way," the chubby boy said. "Without me, we'd never have found such a good spot to stay in Mystic."

"We?" said Frank. "Since when have you been eager to go on a trip that might prove dangerous?"

"Oh," Chet answered, "I think we can be cautious enough to avoid danger, but the big thing is that one of the best scrimshaw collections in the United States is located at the museum in Mystic. And I'm not going to miss that, let me tell you."

"To say nothing of Mrs. Snow's kitchen abilities," Joe added.

"That is an extra incentive," Chet admitted.

Before he drove off in his jalopy, the boys decided to depart for Mystic the day after next.

"I'll be ready!" Chet promised. Frank and Joe stood grinning a moment as the jalopy backfired its way down the street and disappeared, then they went inside.

Joe raided the refrigerator and the boys had a short snack before they went to bed.

Early the following morning they began making preparations for the trip. First they called Biff and Tony and asked them to fill in as carnival sleuths until they returned.

Biff and Tony promised they would and said they would begin their duties as soon as the carnival opened for the day. Then Joe called Solo, who agreed to the change and wished the Hardys luck in their hunt for the mysterious person known as Beluga.

"Mr. Solo said the arrangement would be fine," Joe told his brother.

"Good," Frank said with an air of abstraction. He was staring out the window and his brow was wrinkled. Suddenly he snapped his fingers. "Wow!" he said. "What an idea I just got to smoke out our enemies!"

CHAPTER IX

A Decoy Report

JOE responded to Frank's plan with enthusiasm and the boys hastened to Chief Collig to secure his cooperation. After they had exchanged greetings and were seated across the desk from Collig, Frank said, "Chief, Joe and I have a favor to ask of you."

Collig folded his hands. "I'm always willing to listen."

"We'd like to have you arrange for a phony news item to appear in the evening papers."

Collig raised his eyebrows. "A phony item?"

"Yes," Frank said. "A story reporting that Joe and I found the stolen balloons and have figured out how the theft was managed."

"Nothing untrue in that," Collig stated.

"But that's only the first part of the story," Frank went on. "In the second part, we want it stated that we've discovered the *precise* location of the whale, and that as soon as we've recovered it,

73

we're going to set up another colossal whale show."

Collig thought for a moment, then asked, "What do you think a story like this will accomplish?"

"I'm convinced," Frank answered, "that some of the carnival people are in this, but I suspect quite strongly that they're not the only ones. I feel there's a good chance this ruse might smoke them out into the open."

"It's possible," Collig agreed. "But you're aware, aren't you, that you'll be setting yourselves up as targets? If you're right in thinking the whale's been lost, those crooks might well come after you."

"We realize that," Joe said. "We'll be on guard."

Chief Collig doodled on a scratch pad while he reflected. After a minute's silence he said, "Well, it does look like our best course of action. If you boys promise to stay alert, I'll arrange to have the story put into the paper."

"Thanks, Chief," Frank said and stood up. "I have a hunch we're going to get some results."

The boys left the police station and drove out to the carnival. Biff and Tony were on the job. Since everything was running smoothly, the Hardys stayed only for a few minutes of social conversation and then returned home. They started to pack, and when that was finished, they studied road maps to select the best route from Bayport to Mystic.

Their mother and Aunt Gertrude had taken Cousin Elmer out to see the sights of Bayport, and the afternoon crept by at a turtle's pace. Finally at five o'clock they sauntered down to a stationery store a few blocks from their home.

Gus, the balding proprietor, waved to them when they entered. "Hi, Frank. Hi, Joe. See you got your names in the papers."

"Oh?" Joe feigned surprise.

"Yeah. Right there on page one. Ain't you seen it yet?"

"No," Frank said. "Where?"

Gus scooped up the top paper from a stack of fresh deliveries and spread it open on the counter. He jabbed a story with his finger. "See? Right there. *'Bayport Sleuths Solve Riddle of Missing Whale,'* it says. Boy, that was pretty fast work. You guys are sure good."

"Oh, no!" Frank groaned as he scanned the item.

"What's the matter?" Joe asked.

"They've printed the whole story," Frank replied.

"What's wrong?" Gus inquired. "You guys act like something terrible's happened."

"I don't know how this paper got hold of the story," Frank said. "But by running it, they've tipped our hand."

"What do you mean?"

"We didn't want anyone to know we'd located the whale until we were ready to make our move," Joe said. "The time isn't right yet. We still have a few things to do."

Gus scratched his head. "Sorry they jumped the gun, but you guys cracked this case in fine time. You got every reason to be proud."

"Thanks, Gus," Frank said.

The Hardys paid for the paper and left the store. Walking home, Frank said, "I really hated to fool Gus like that, but if anyone does some checking, our story will hold up."

Joe nodded. "We can set things right with Gus later. He'll understand."

The boys reached home to find that the others had returned. Cousin Elmer, who claimed that his sea legs were not up to so much walking, had gone to his room for a nap. Frank and Joe showed the news item to their mother and Aunt Gertrude and explained their plan.

Aunt Gertrude's hand flew to her throat. "Oh, land's sake! What have you boys done!"

"It's all right, Aunty," Frank said. "Joe and I'll be ready for anything."

"But those are dangerous criminals," Miss Hardy wailed.

Joe patted her hand. "Aunty," he said soothingly, "you've never known us to be reckless, right? Well, we don't intend to change now. Dad's working on a tight schedule and every moment counts."

Mrs. Hardy, too, was worried about the boys, but she had confidence in their resources and abilities. "They will do all right, Gertrude," she said.

The phone rang. It was the Bayport branch office of a national television network. The TV news interviewer asked Frank to comment on the story and to give him additional information if possible.

"Well," said Frank, "we didn't want the news to break this early, but as long as it has, there's nothing we can do about it. Yes, it's true. All I can tell you is that we'll pick up the whale when the time is right—which shouldn't be long."

A second call, this one from a local radio station, followed on the heels of the first. And so it went for the rest of the evening. Joe and Frank took turns answering the inquiries, and by the time they were ready for bed, they had spoken to representatives of more than half of the major radio and television networks and all of the local stations.

Chet arrived early the next morning. In addition to his plaid zippered suitcase he carried a small black leather case.

"Hey, doc," Joe said jokingly, "got all your instruments?"

"Why'd you bring that?" added Frank. "For house calls?"

"You're both pretty nosy," Chet said mysteriously. "I'll tell you what's in this later."

The Hardys said their good-bys and were on the road shortly before nine o'clock. They listened to a newscast on the car radio and were pleased to hear the details of the story they had planted.

"If this doesn't bring our enemies out," Frank said, "then nothing will."

It was a fine, bright day. The highway was relatively free of traffic and the travelers made good time. They had been driving for two hours when they heard the wail of a police siren approaching them from behind.

At the wheel, Frank spotted the State Police car in the rear-view mirror. "Boy, he's moving fast. Must be awfully anxious to catch the car he's after."

"It isn't us," Joe remarked. "We're within the speed limit."

Frank edged to the right to allow the police car plenty of room to pass. To his surprise, the trooper motioned for him to pull off the road and stop. Frank complied.

"We're in for it now," Chet fretted. "They're going to arrest you guys for planting a phony news story. And they're going to charge me with being an accomplice!"

"Don't be a worrywart, Chet," Joe said. "We had Chief Collig's permission. It must be something else."

The trooper got out and walked to Frank's open window, the leather of his holster and his highly polished boots gleaming in the sunlight.

"We're in trouble!" Chet lamented. "Look at his face. He means business!"

The trooper consulted his note pad, then asked "Are you Frank and Joe Hardy and Chet Morton?"

"Yes, sir," Frank replied. "What's wrong, Officer?"

"I received radio instructions through Chief Collig's office in Bayport to relay a message to you. Your mother received a call a short while ago in reference to the case you're working on. The man didn't identify himself and his message was short: *'Lady, tell your brats that they'll lay off if they know what's good for 'em!'* "

"Man!" Frank said. "We got through to them. They're really worried now!" He thanked the officer for having delivered the message. The policeman said he was glad to be of help. He cautioned the boys to be on the alert, then he returned to his car and drove off.

The young sleuths maintained maximum vigilance during the remainder of the drive to Mystic. Chet was the only one who noticed anything out of the ordinary. He pointed out a blonde in a red coupé who seemed to have been following them for half an hour. Frank and Joe laughed.

"She's probably going to Mystic, too," Joe said.

"I don't think we have much to fear from a pretty girl. To tell the truth, Chet, I think you're just looking for an excuse to flirt."

Chet blushed, mumbled, and looked straight ahead for the next five miles.

By the time they arrived in Mystic, it was mid-afternoon. Joe took a map of the town from the glove compartment and directed Frank toward Mrs. Snow's house.

Suddenly there was the roar of an accelerating engine behind them. The same red coupé went shooting past, cut sharply in front of them, and forced Frank off the street and over the curb.

The windshield was filled with the sight of a huge elm tree. They were heading straight for it!

CHAPTER X

Tim Varney

"Hang on!" Frank shouted.

He slammed the brake pedal down and wrenched the wheel violently to the side. The car went into a skid, tipped precariously up on two wheels, then was brought to a bone-jarring halt when the right fender buckled against the tree.

"Anybody hurt?" Frank gasped.

"I'm okay," Joe said.

"Me too," Chet answered shakily.

"Lucky we had our seat belts fastened," Frank said.

"There is no doubt that our enemies are here," Joe muttered. "That blonde certainly was no lady."

"She may come back to find out what happened to us," Frank remarked. "Mrs. Snow's house should be right down at the end of this block.

Let's get there fast, conceal the car, and keep a lookout."

"Good thinking," Joe said.

"I'm all for concealment at this stage of the game," Chet added.

After a quick check, which revealed that the only damage was the crumpled fender, Frank drove to Mrs. Snow's house and parked in her driveway. The boys hurried up the front steps and rang the bell.

Mrs. Snow, a small, white-haired woman, opened the door. The boys introduced themselves hurriedly and told of what had just happened.

"Why, the nerve of those scoundrels!" Mrs. Snow replied. "Joe and Chet, come right inside. Frank, you can take your car around back and park it in the garage."

Frank drove into the rickety clapboard garage behind the house and closed the door. When he turned to go back into the house, he saw the tail end of a red car whizzing by.

"Wow!" he said softly to himself. "She certainly came back in a hurry!"

He raced in to join the others. "Did you see—?" he started, but Joe interrupted him.

"Negative. It was not the same car. We'll have to wait, I'm afraid."

The trio and Mrs. Snow stood alongside the front windows, keeping vigil at the edges of the drawn curtains.

"Aha!" Joe said ten minutes later. "Here comes the coupé."

"Are you sure it's the right car?" Chet asked.

"I'm not likely to forget that one for a long time."

The red automobile was moving slowly down the street. As it passed in front of Mrs. Snow's house, the sleuths noticed that there were now three people in it.

"She must have picked up some confederates," Joe said.

"Do you recognize any of them?" Frank asked Mrs. Snow, who stood at his elbow.

"I never saw the girl," she replied. "But I've seen the big man, the one in the blue work shirt. I'm not sure, but I think he's a retired seaman."

Unfortunately the boys could not get a really clear look. To do so, they would have had to open the curtains and possibly give away their position. The car passed by the house twice again in the next fifteen minutes, then vanished.

"I think our trip is *really* going to pay off," Frank announced. He asked Mrs. Snow if he might use her telephone to make a long-distance collect call. She led him to the phone table in the hall.

Frank had the operator ring his home in Bayport. Elmer Hardy answered, accepted the charge, and told Frank that his mother and aunt were out. Frank asked him to report that he had received

Mrs. Hardy's message and everything was all right.

Elmer said there had been no word from Mr. Hardy yet and that none of Chief Collig's men had been able to uncover any news about Boko. Frank thanked Elmer and hung up.

The boys decided to remain at Mrs. Snow's, since there seemed to be little they could accomplish the rest of the day. Mrs. Snow showed them to their rooms, and while they unpacked, she went downstairs and had supper waiting by the time they reappeared.

The boys slept well that night in spacious, comfortable beds. They got an early start in the morning and arrived at the museum just as it was opening.

"We'll case the area first," Frank said, and warned Chet to act casual. "And if you see the blonde," he added, "for Pete's sake, don't sing out!"

They bided their time, strolling through the streets and visiting the period buildings. The Hardys took particular delight in the dark and triangular Shipsmith Shop and the relaxing, convivial atmosphere of the Spouter Tavern. Chet's chief interest lay in the many beautiful pieces contained in the separate collections of scrimshaw in the museum.

Around eleven o'clock they strolled toward the wharf at which the old whaling ship *Charles W.*

Morgan was moored. A group of leathery-skinned men in seamen's garb was congregated on a nearby bench.

"That fellow in the blue shirt," Frank whispered to Joe and Chet. "Isn't he one of the guys who was in the red car?"

Chet and Joe admitted there was a strong resemblance, but could not be sure.

Frank decided to strike up a conversation with the man while the other two went aboard the whaler. He sauntered to the bench and sat down.

"What a beautiful ship," he said. "I'll bet she has quite a history."

"Aye. She does," replied the man in the blue shirt.

"I'd sure like to go through her with someone who could tell me her background," Frank went on.

"I'll take you—for a dollar!"

"It's a deal." Frank took a bill from his wallet and handed it to the grizzled man.

"Thanks. Tim's the name."

Frank's heart quickened as he saw a whale tattoo, similar to Boko's on his guide's blue-veined hand.

The two quickly boarded the *Charles W. Morgan*, and walked past Joe and Chet, who were chatting with a man in a captain's uniform. Tim took Frank on a quick tour of the deck. He knew his subject well, pointing out the davits from which the longboats were lowered to pursue whales, the brick hearths over which the oil was boiled from the blubber, and explained the function of the huge pieces of block and tackle.

As the old fellow expounded, Frank noticed that Chet and Joe were now following him at a discreet distance.

Tim took Frank below deck, where the enormous backbone of a Bowhead Whale was propped against the ribs of the ship. The two moved in its direction, while Tim explained how the ship's frame and planking had been built of live oak. He pointed out the broad-bladed harpoons used for the original strike against a whale and the thinner, long-shanked iron lances employed in the final killing thrust to the heart.

An old anchor chain lay in a great coil near the tall, gleaming white backbone. Frank bent down to examine the chain's massive links.

"Do you mean," he said, "that they really cranked something this heavy up by—?"

His question was cut short by a grating sound. He jerked his eyes up and saw the backbone falling on him. Instantly he hurled himself backward, hit the deck, and rolled away. The heavy whalebone crashed over the coiled chain!

Joe and Chet came pounding to his side as he regained his feet. "Frank! Frank! Are you all right?" his brother asked.

"Yes. It missed. Quick, where did Tim go?"

Instantly Frank hurled himself backward

"He ran up that gangway," Chet cried. "Right after he shoved the backbone at you."

"After him!" Frank commanded.

The boys dashed up the steps to the upper deck. The area was jammed with tourists and also the wharf below.

"Too late," Joe said angrily. "We'd never find him in this crowd."

The boys leaned against a rail. "We know his full name at least," Joe said.

Frank looked surprised. "How so?"

"From Captain Flint," Joe explained. "It's Tim Varney."

Frank nodded approvingly. "Nice work, Joe." He told them about Varney's whale tattoo, and suggested they talk to Captain Flint again.

Flint was outraged that such a thing had happened on his ship, and apologized to Frank. "I wish I could tell you more about Varney," he said, "but I can't. Nobody around here knows anything about him, except that he's a drifter."

"Captain," Joe asked, "are you familiar with stuffed whales?"

The captain pursed his lips. "Well, there's only one that I've ever heard of. It's in a museum of natural history. Wait a minute. There's somebody who knows more about this than I do."

He walked to the prow of the ship and hailed an old man seated on one of the benches, sunning himself.

"Oh, Murphy!" Captain Flint called out. "Will you come over here, please."

The man, gray and toothless, waved in reply and walked up to the whaler. "You want something, Captain?"

Flint cupped his hands and asked the question about stuffed whales.

"Sure, I know another one," Murphy replied. "It was washed ashore on Montauk in the 1920's. Some carnival guy stuffed it."

"You know his name or where I can find him?" Frank asked. But the old man shook his head, and shuffled back to his bench.

"That's a great help, Captain," Frank said. "Another question. Have you ever heard of a man named Whitey Meldrum?"

"Whitey Meldrum? Sure. He's an old merchant marine seaman. I don't know the specifics, but he was mixed up in a couple of shady deals several years back."

"You have any idea where he is now?"

Captain Flint removed his hat and scratched his head. "I'm not sure, but I seem to remember someone mentioning that he was living in New York. That was about two months ago."

"Captain," Frank said, "you've been a tremendous help to us and I want to thank you very much."

"Not at all. My pleasure. Oh, there's one more thing."

"Yes?"

"I just recalled. Strange thing, you looking for Meldrum. There was another fellow up here just a couple of days ago. He was looking for old Meldrum, too."

"Who was he?" Joe asked.

"Marlin. Called himself Spike Marlin."

CHAPTER XI

The Eavesdroppers

"ARE you joking?" Joe asked. "Spike Marlin. Turn it around and you get marlinespike, the tool used in rope splicing."

"It struck me the same way," Captain Flint replied. "But that's what he said his name was."

"Fine alias for a guy with a sense of humor," Frank said, and asked the captain where Marlin was from or where he was going. Flint did not know. "Was there anything unusual about him, anything that might help us to identify him?" Frank asked.

"Not much. His clothes were worn, but pretty nondescript. I did notice an anchor tattoo on the back of his left hand. He might have been a seaman, but I wouldn't swear to it."

"Those are pretty good clues," Joe said. "Thanks a lot."

The boys left to scan the area, trying to pick up Tim Varney's trail. They had no luck, so they returned to Mrs. Snow's in the late afternoon. After supper they headed back to the seaport.

They searched in seamen's meeting houses and in cheap restaurants, and questioned proprietors of stores and clerks at hotel desks. But their efforts were fruitless. Several persons readily admitted to knowing Varney, but no one had seen him for the last few days or knew where he might be found.

Finally the trio stopped at a drugstore and ordered sodas.

"Boy, these are really good!" Joe said after the first cooling gulp.

"*Good!* My friend, they're superb!" Chet responded. He finished his soda before the Hardys were halfway done and ordered another. After the gurgling sound of the straw reaching bottom, Chet gave the Hardys a plaintive look. "Fellows," he said, "it's not that I'm trying to get out of work or anything, but these sodas are the best I've ever tasted."

"What are you trying to say, Chet?" Joe asked.

The chubby boy wore a sheepish expression. "Well, if you guys think you might be able to do without me for a while, I'd sure like to stick around and do some real justice to that artist who makes these ice-cream dreams."

"Look, Chet," Joe said. "We were planning on having you lead us in a couple of double-time laps around the block."

Chet raised his hands in mock horror, and

Frank added, "Okay. If we run into any trouble, we'll come back and get you. Otherwise plan on meeting us here in an hour."

Frank and Joe left the drugstore and continued their search. Darkness was falling and the moon was visible only as a dim, thin crescent above a layer of black wind-driven clouds.

"Do you think Tim Varney has gone into hiding?" Joe asked.

"It's a possibility. I— Wait a minute! Over there by the grocery store, Joe!"

Joe squinted against the blackness, focusing his eyes on the figure that was moving furtively along the other side of the street. "That's our man, all right."

"Into this doorway, quick," Frank said. "Give him a chance to get a bit of a lead, then we'll follow him."

Varney glanced nervously around, as if to make sure that he was not being followed. After a moment he shrugged and hurried on. When he was half a block away, Frank and Joe stepped out of the doorway. They tailed the man through a labyrinth of twisting streets until he arrived at a clapboard shack close to the waterfront. Varney paused, looked around him, then pulled open the door and went inside.

Frank and Joe pressed against the side of a warehouse, watching. "What do you think we should do now?" Joe asked.

"Well," Frank said, "there was no light when he entered, and he still hasn't turned one on. It's my guess that he's waiting for somebody. I think we should stick tight and see what happens."

"Okay."

After fifteen minutes Joe grew restless and began to fidget, when Frank suddenly whispered, "Something's moving off to the side of the shack."

Joe looked. Two dark forms—one of them much larger than the other—were approaching the ramshackle structure. They made their way to the door, then rapped on it with four sharp knocks. The door opened and they stepped inside. Moments later a weak light appeared behind the covered windows.

The boys crouched low and covered the distance between the shack and the warehouse at a half-run. A thin wedge of light knifed through a crack on the side of the door. The Hardys each pressed an eye to the opening.

Inside, three men were pacing about. One of them strode close to the door. Instantly Frank and Joe recognized him as the hulking man who had been in the red coupé with Varney and the blonde.

"Hey, Mug!" came Varney's voice.

The big man turned. "What?"

The boys could not make out Varney's next sentence. A higher voice said, "Wish we could get this job finished." Frank and Joe strained for a look at the speaker. Moments later they succeeded, when a youth about their own age, slightly built and with sandy hair, stomped angrily past the door, snarling the name "Hardy."

"There's nothin' you can do, Baby Face!"

"Well, I don't like sittin' around, Mug," replied the blond youth hotly. "There's no sense talkin' any more. Let's get out of this hole."

He strode toward the door, barely giving Frank and Joe time to scoot around the corner of the shack. The light went out, the door slammed shut, and the three vanished into the darkness.

Frank peered around the corner in time to see two headlights wink on, a motor start, and a car pull away.

"Nuts, we can't follow them," he muttered.

Joe grabbed his arm. "Remember that night I saw someone lurking near the phone booth at the carnival?"

"Yes."

"Well, that fellow Baby Face is the one I saw hanging around there."

Frank raised his eyebrows. "This gets more interesting—and complicated—every moment."

"There's no doubt that Varney was trying to split your skull on the whaler," Joe said. "But just what do you think is this job they're talking about?"

"I don't know. It could be connected with the stolen whale, or it might have something to do with Dad's case."

"Or both cases, for that matter," Joe added.

"Right, but remember we still don't have one shred of positive proof. Originally we thought the whale had been stolen by someone from the carnival. Now suddenly we find this fair-haired guy was at the carnival, which, while not ruling out the carnival people, seems to imply a bigger gang. Also there's that postcard signed Beluga that was mailed from here."

"And once we got to Mystic," Joe said, "we started running into seamen who are involved—Tim Varney and Whitey Meldrum. The gang Dad is after is made up of seamen. Wow! What a mess! Frank, I think we should get the police to arrest these guys right now."

"No good, Joe. There's nothing they can be charged with—at the moment."

"Varney tried to smash you with that whalebone!"

"He could claim it was an accident, and we couldn't prove otherwise."

"Well, I still think we should get them while we have the chance," Joe said.

"They'd only be set free ten minutes after the police brought them in," Frank countered, "and besides, they're not sure how much we know about them. We'd be tipping our hand. Come on. Let's investigate this shack!"

They walked in. Joe struck a match and lit the wick of the old-fashioned lamp.

Two things instantly captured their attention—a woman's blond wig and a souvenir cane from Solo's Super Carnival!

CHAPTER XII

An Odd Messenger

JOE picked up the wig and turned it over in his hands. "You know, when Chet said 'That was no lady' he didn't know just how right he was!"

"Baby Face in disguise," Frank muttered. "He and I are going to have a few things to settle when we finally come face to face."

Joe set down the wig on the cane, which he twirled a moment like a baton. "This proves that at least one of them if not all three were at the carnival."

They went through the rest of the shack, but discovered no additional clues.

"We still don't know Beluga's real name," Frank said tersely.

"Or what his game is," Joe added.

Frank's brow wrinkled as he repeated the message Beluga had sent to Boko. " '*Getting hot. Get-*

ting hot.' It could mean a couple of things. For instance, 'We're almost to our goal.' Or, 'The police are close on our trail.' "

The boys pondered the possibilities. Finally Joe said, "I think we've done about as much as we can do here. What do you say we go back for Chet?"

Frank glanced at his watch. "Okay. The hour's just about up to meet Chet." They hastened off. Reaching the drugstore, the Hardys saw nearly a dozen youths clustered around the soda counter, talking excitedly.

"C'mon, boy. You can do it!"

"Just take it slow and easy."

"No problem, fellow. Still plenty of room left."

"Go for broke, champ!"

The Hardys made their way forward and discovered the object of everyone's attention—Chet Morton! He grinned weakly when he saw his pals. "Hi, Frank. Hi, Joe."

"What are you doing, Chet?" Frank asked.

"Competing in a marathon." Chet made a sweeping gesture with his hand, taking in a row of empty soda glasses.

Joe counted. "Five! You put down five sodas?"

"You bet he did," said a girl at Joe's elbow. "And he's far from finished!"

"That's right," agreed a boy. "The big one's still ahead of him."

"You see," Chet said, "I've never encountered such scrumptious sodas in my life, and before I knew it—well, I knocked off five of them. And now, Charlie . . . Oh, excuse me. Frank and Joe, I'd like you to meet Charlie, a soda-making genius!"

The man behind the counter smiled. "Your friend here is a marvel. I've never seen anybody put 'em away like him."

"That's the problem," Chet explained. "Charlie was so impressed that he offered me a King-Size Wonder—that's his specialty—on the house. I'm not sure I can handle it, but I just can't bring myself to turn it down!"

As the crowd chattered encouragingly, Frank and Joe shook their heads in amazement. "How do you do it, Chet?" Frank asked. "How in *the world* do you do it?"

"I have a natural talent," Chet replied modestly.

"Well, what's it going to be?" Charlie asked cheerfully. "A King-Size Wonder or defeat?"

Chet gnawed on his lower lip. A freckled redhead clapped him on the back. "Hey, buddy, I got an idea. Why don't you take a couple of spins around the block. That'll work off some of the sodas you've already had, and give you the room you need to take on the big baby."

Chet contemplated this a moment, then smiled and stood up. "Ordinarily," he said, "I shun physical exercise. But this is a worthy cause and I feel that a sacrifice is in order."

"That's the spirit," Charlie said.

Chet walked out of the drugstore. He stood on the sidewalk, hitched up his pants, and rubbed his hands together. A determined look settled over his face, then he jogged down the block. The freckle-faced boy and another fan went with him.

Ten minutes and two laps later, Chet returned to his stool in front of the counter. Charlie had the King-Size Wonder waiting. It was a huge soda, made with four flavors of ice cream and enhanced with a great variety of nuts and fruits. A large mound of whipped cream topped it and a bright-red cherry sat at the peak of the whipped cream. The audience murmured appreciatively.

Chet picked up his spoon, looked around like a matador, then tackled the soda. His fans cheered as he ate with a slow, steady rhythm. When he reached the halfway mark, the spectators began to applaud. The sound of their clapping hands grew progressively louder as the tubby boy neared the end, then broke into a wild crescendo when Chet scooped out the last bit of ice cream.

"I wouldn't have believed it if I hadn't seen it," Frank said.

Chet's admirers followed the boys out of the store, congratulating him heartily. A block and a half later the last of the fans fell away. Chet sighed and patted his stomach. "A truly inspiring experience," he said.

Frank and Joe could do nothing but express

their awe. Then the subject turned to what had happened at the shack. "So that cute blonde of yours," Frank finished, "was none other than Baby Face!"

"Oh, no!" Chet exclaimed. Then he said quickly, "I almost forgot. I have some news for you, too."

"What?" Frank asked.

"Knocker Felsen's in Mystic. He's looking for you."

"You're kidding!" Joe exploded.

"No I'm not."

"What's he want?" Frank asked.

"I don't know. He wouldn't say. But I told him he could find us at Mrs. Snow's house."

"Oh, that's great!" Joe said. "Didn't you stop to think that Felsen may be a member of the gang we're after?"

Chet looked embarrassed. Apparently this possibility had not occurred to him. "I'm sorry, fellows. Since he came looking for you right out in the open . . ." He held his hands up helplessly.

"What's done is done," Frank remarked. "I think we should play it cool and approach Mrs. Snow's place indirectly, in case Felsen is up to something sneaky."

Three blocks from Mrs. Snow's house the boys took to back yards and advanced stealthily. Reaching Mrs. Snow's property, they split up to reconnoiter, agreeing to meet again behind a large clump of lilac bushes.

Joe was the first to spot Felsen. He was hiding behind a tree close to Mrs. Snow's back porch. The three boys knelt at the base of the lilac bushes. "Here's what we'll do," Frank whispered. "Joe and I will circle around and come at him from both sides. Chet, you stay out of the action. If Joe and I run into more than we can handle, you pitch in."

The boys moved out and began creeping toward their positions. When they were set, Frank whistled shrilly and rushed forward. He and Joe reached Felsen at the same moment and the three went down with a thud.

Felsen recovered from the surprise attack quickly and jammed an elbow into Frank's stomach, knocking the wind out of him. He threw Joe off and made a rush toward a neighbor's yard. Joe was after him in a flash, bringing the burly carny to earth with a flying tackle. Frank scrambled to his hands and knees, rested a moment until he got his breath back, then rushed into the fray just as Felsen was struggling to his feet. *Pow!* A right to the chin flattened the big youth.

"Okay, tough guy," Frank said, pulling the groggy Felsen to his feet. "Let's have some explanations."

Felsen pressed a handkerchief to his bleeding

nose. "Look, you guys, I'm not your enemy. Why'd you jump me like that?"

"Why were you skulking behind that tree?" Chet asked, stepping forward.

"Mr. Solo sent me to give you a message. He told me you were on a tricky case and that I was supposed to be careful."

"Okay," Joe said. "What's the message?"

"The carnival's closing in Bayport. We made as much as we can there and we're moving on to Newton."

Newton was a small town thirty-five miles from Bayport. Neither Frank, Joe, nor Chet could understand why Solo would send Felsen all the way to Mystic just to inform them of the move.

"Was there anything else?" Joe asked.

"Yeah. A note." Felsen went through his pockets. A worried expression came over his face. "I must have lost it!" he exclaimed.

The boys searched the ground, but found nothing. Then Knocker explained that he had planned to return to Bayport earlier that evening. "I can't go now," he said dejectedly. "It's too late."

"Where will you sleep?" Chet asked him.

"Don't know. Could I stay with you guys?"

Frank was suspicious and far from pleased at the prospect. Joe felt the same way. Chet, however, felt that Knocker was okay.

"All right, you can stay with us," Frank said finally. "But no funny business!"

Felsen was given a cot and fell asleep quickly, and the Hardys and Chet followed suit shortly.

At daybreak Frank suddenly snapped awake and glanced about. Felsen's cot was empty! He leaped up and roused Chet and Joe. Neither of them had heard Felsen leave.

Frank sat down on the cot. "I knew this would happen. Hey, what's this?" He reached down and drew an object from within a fold in the covers. "Felsen's wallet!"

The three of them examined the wallet carefully and Frank located a cleverly concealed secret compartment. From it he drew out a folded piece of paper which he opened.

It was a pencil drawing of a man's fist. At the base of the thumb, and on the tip and the base of the index finger were three sections of a tattoo, which, when joined, formed a whale!

CHAPTER XIII

A Great Surprise

"WHAT do you think of Knocker Felsen now, Chet?" Frank asked.

"Can't win 'em all," Chet said apologetically.

There was a knock on the door. "Come in," Joe called out.

The door opened and there, out of breath, stood Knocker Felsen. The three boys regarded him in stunned silence.

"Man," said Felsen, "I was just getting on my bus when I discovered I'd lost my wallet. Did you see it laying around anywhere?"

"Yes," Frank answered. "And we also found this!" He confronted Felsen with the whale tattoo.

"What's that?" Felsen asked.

"You tell us," Frank replied. "We found it in your wallet. And say, why'd you sneak off like that?"

"Didn't want to disturb you," Felsen said. He

eyed the note. "Hey, that's what Mr. Solo gave me to deliver to you. He found it near Rembrandt's bunk and he thinks it might be a clue. Am I glad it wasn't lost after all."

Frank eyed Felsen with distrust. "Well, thanks anyway. And say thanks to Mr. Solo, too."

Felsen took his wallet and left, grumbling all the way out. The boys waited until his voice faded before they spoke.

"What do you think?" Joe asked.

Frank sighed. "I don't really know. He might be telling the truth and he might not. Too many unknowns to start drawing conclusions."

"I wonder if we might get anywhere trying to trace the Long Island whale that Murphy told us about," Joe said.

"I was thinking along that same line," Frank remarked. "I suggest we look through the old newspaper files in the New York Public Library."

Both Hardys looked to Chet for confirmation. He shrugged his big shoulders. "It's okay with me. I'm just the Indian. You guys are the chiefs."

They packed their bags and went downstairs. Mrs. Snow served them breakfast in the dining room. The boys ate, thanked her for her help and hospitality, settled their account and left.

The drive to New York City was long and uneventful, and the boys took turns at the wheel. They arrived in the midafternoon, parked near Times Square, and walked the few blocks to the main branch of the library. It was a huge, imposing building. The long flight of stairs that rose to its main entrance was guarded by two stone lions.

The boys went directly to the section in which the microfilm copies of old newspapers were kept. They checked out the indexes of the various New York papers for the years 1919 through 1929. Frank, Joe, and Chet each took a third of the material to be perused, sat down, and began poring through the thick volumes.

Other patrons of the library came and went, as the large clock on the wall silently marked the passage of time.

Joe marked his place, looked up, and stretched. Suddenly he went rigid. Across the room and seated at a table pretending he was reading a newspaper was Baby Face! Without taking his eyes from the youth, Joe reached over and tapped his brother's arm.

At that moment Baby Face looked up. Joe noticed two things in the split second that followed. First, the man's shocked look of panic at having been recognized—and second, a black circular mole just above the bridge of his nose and directly between his eyes.

Baby Face was the first to move. He leaped from his chair and bolted out of the room. Frank and Joe were after him in a flash. They hesitated when they reached the hall. Including the up and the down stairwells, there were five possible directions in which Baby Face could have gone.

A guard came up to them. "Here, here! You can't run through the library making a racket like this!"

"We're chasing a criminal," Joe explained. "A young man, short and slightly built, with sandy hair. Did you see him?"

"No. I just came out of the manuscript room."

Frank's shoulders slumped. "I'm afraid we're out of luck, Joe. There are too many directions he could have taken. We'd never find him."

Frank and Joe apologized for the disturbance and returned to the newspaper section. Chet looked up when they approached. "Where did you guys go? You took off like rockets before I even knew what was happening."

The Hardys told him about Baby Face spying on them and of how they were unable to catch him.

"Well, it's not a total loss," Chet said. "While you were gone I found this." He turned the index in his hands around so that they could read it and pointed to a specific entry:

WHALE. Discovered off Montauk Point. May 14, 1924. Section III, p. 15, col. A

"Good work, Chet," Frank said. "Now we're getting somewhere."

They requested the appropriate roll of micro-film and put it into the viewing machine. Frank worked the crank handle until he located the page they wanted. Chet and Joe pressed in on either side of him. It was not a very long story, but it did confirm that the stranded giant was indeed a Blue Whale and that it had been sold to Ralph Zele-meyer—owner of Zelemeyer's Circus—who intended to have it stuffed and to use it as a side-show attraction.

The boys returned the microfilm to the librarian. They decided to sit in the park behind the library a while, have an ice-cream bar, and discuss what they had learned. New York City's businesses were closing and the park was crowded. The boys strolled through it, seeking an unoccupied bench.

"I don't think there's any doubt that the Montauk whale is the same one Biff and Tony discovered," Frank said. "The next step is to locate Zelemeyer's Circus."

"As long as we're in New York," Joe suggested, "why don't we skip the circus a while and try to run down Whitey Meldrum?"

"That sounds reasonable," Frank agreed.

"Hey, fellows," Chet said, "I hate to spoil a good ice-cream bar, but there are some not-too-friendly friends of ours over there."

Frank and Joe looked in the direction Chet indicated. Near a water fountain they saw Baby Face talking to Tim Varney.

Frank flung his ice cream into a trash basket and sprinted forward. "Let's go!"

Chet and Joe were right behind him. Their dash was like running an army obstacle course. They had to thread their way through knots of people and careen around others. Baby Face and Tim Varney spotted them coming.

"It's the brats!" Varney yelled. "We gotta scram!"

The criminals ran out of the park and plunged into a subway entrance. Frank, Joe, and Chet followed them, but three minutes of search in the jammed labyrinth were futile. They emerged disappointed.

"Let's hope we have better luck with Meldrum," Joe said.

After Frank had consulted his notebook for the addresses of three homes for old seamen that Captain Flint had given them, the boys were lucky enough to find a taxi in the rush-hour traffic.

Frank gave the driver the first address. Half an hour later they pulled up in front of a three-story brick building with white shutters and wrought-iron grillwork.

A plaque set into the cornerstone identified it as *Seamen's Haven*.

The boys entered the building and went to the

clerk's desk. "Excuse me," said Frank. "We're looking for an old merchant sailor by the name of Whitey Meldrum. Does he live here by any chance?"

"He used to," the clerk replied. "Took off 'bout a week ago. Don't know when he's comin' back—if ever!"

"Boy, what a sense of timing we have," Joe said. "Say, would you have a guest here by the name of Spike Marlin?"

"Matter of fact, we do. Checked in a couple of days after Meldrum left. Friend of Meldrum's. What do you want with him?"

"We—er—have some mutual acquaintances. We promised them we'd look old Spike up."

The clerk shrugged. "He's in room 2-D. Up the stairs and to your left. Second floor."

"Thanks," Frank said.

Grinning with excited anticipation, the three ascended the stairs, walked softly down the hall, and stopped in front of 2-D.

Frank put an ear to the door and listened for a while. Someone was moving quietly about. Since there was no conversation, Frank assumed the person inside was alone. He stepped back and beckoned to the others.

"We don't know what to expect," Frank whispered, "so let's be ready for anything. Joe, you and Chet each get on one side of the door. I'll knock. Ready?"

Frank whispered, "Let's be ready for anything!"

Chet and Joe took up their positions and nodded. Frank tensed his muscles and prepared himself for instant action. He clenched his hand into a fist and rapped loudly upon the door.

Silence. Frank knocked again, this time even louder.

"Just a minute," came the muffled reply.

Footsteps approached, then the door was flung open. A well-built man stood before them.

Frank's eyes bulged and his jaw dropped. "Dad!" he gasped.

CHAPTER XIV

An Airport Snatch

"FRANK!" exclaimed Mr. Hardy in astonishment. "What in the world are you doing here?"

The detective was even more amazed when Chet and Joe stepped into view. He glanced up and down the hall to make sure no one had witnessed the meeting, then beckoned the boys inside.

Mr. Hardy was dressed in old work clothes. His hair was dyed gray and his face made up to look old. Though the masquerade was effective, Frank and Joe would have recognized their father's tall figure and handsome countenance anywhere.

"Don't tell us you got tattooed just to make your disguise authentic!" Frank said, looking at the blue anchor on the back of Fenton Hardy's left hand.

The sleuth laughed. "No, it's only a semipermanent ink. It'll wash out with a few good scrubbings."

"Spike Marlin, what a name!" Joe grinned. "Takes real talent to make that up!"

"Don't you know you're looking at a genius?" his father quipped.

When the boys made themselves comfortable, Frank asked what connection Whitey Meldrum had with the Ivory Idol.

His father explained, "The back of the envelope in which the letter to R. R. Dunn was sent was sealed with cellophane tape. I managed to take a good thumbprint from the tape. It proved to be Meldrum's. Now, may I ask what interest you boys have in our elusive Mr. Meldrum?"

Joe told about the scrap of paper bearing Meldrum's name which had been found in Boko's wagon.

"That links Meldrum pretty well with Boko," Mr. Hardy said. "And probably a man named Tim Varney, too."

"Tim Varney!" Frank exclaimed. "How does he fit into your case?"

"I'm not sure yet. All I know for certain is that Meldrum left here in a hurry after an argument with Tim Varney."

Excitedly the brothers filled their father in on all they knew about Tim Varney and his confederates.

"It's beginning to look more and more as if

there's only *one* case, and not two, as we thought at first," Frank noted.

"That's a very strong possibility," Fenton Hardy agreed.

"Well, what do we do next?" Joe asked.

Mr. Hardy smiled. "I think the most pressing matter at hand is to get some supper."

"Hear! Hear!" Chet said. The Hardys laughed and the quartet walked down the stairs.

"Your friends found you okay—huh, Spike?" the clerk commented.

"Yeah," Mr. Hardy replied in a gruff voice. "Thanks for sendin' 'em up."

"Sure thing."

A sallow-faced man appeared behind the clerk, a dirty duffel bag in his hands. "Hey," he said, "what am I supposed to do with these old shirts of Meldrum's?"

"I don't know," the clerk answered. "Maybe we should dump 'em. We ain't runnin' a storehouse."

"Did you say that duffel belongs to Whitey?" Mr. Hardy asked.

"Yeah. It's full of dirty shirts."

"Look," said the detective. "No sense in dumpin' 'em. I'll keep 'em until ol' Whitey comes back."

The clerk took the duffel and plopped it on the counter. "Help yourself."

Mr. Hardy picked up the bag and casually went back up the stairs. The boys followed. Once back inside 2-D, they locked the door and took the duffel over to the bed.

"Cross your fingers, boys," Mr. Hardy said. "If we're lucky, we might pick up a clue or two." He spilled the shirts onto the spread. There were a dozen of them, several stained and torn. Mr. Hardy and the boys began going through the pockets.

"Here's something!" Chet said. He handed an old faded piece of paper to Mr. Hardy.

The detective studied it and read aloud: " *'It's getting worse every day. Don't know what will happen to Jonah. The Hong Kong job turned out to be a real flop. I'll let you know what happens. J. Kane.'* "

"Wow!" said Joe. "We know now that Kane was one of the thieves who stole the Ivory Idol. But we can't get anything from him. He's dead."

Mr. Hardy was surprised to hear this and continued to search through the rest of the shirts, with negative results. Then, leaving no stone unturned, Frank pulled the duffel bag inside out and examined it. Close to the bottom seam he spotted a line of words in small letters, printed with India ink. "Listen to this!" he said. " *'Society of the Whale Tattoo: Blackright, Beluga, Blue, Bottlenose, and Pygmy.'* "

"That's great, Frank," Mr. Hardy said. "From the thumbprint we know that Meldrum is Black-

right, but who are the others? Tim Varney?
Maybe Boko?"

"And is this really a society?" Joe asked. "Or an
old gang?"

Mr. Hardy became silent. After thinking for a
while, he said, "Frank and Joe, how would you
like to take a fast trip to Los Angeles?"

"Sure," Joe said. "What for?"

"To nail down this Society of the Whale Tattoo. The Los Angeles Police Department has the
most extensive file on tattoos in the world of crim-
inology. They arrest more than two hundred
thousand persons each year, and every tattoo they
find is recorded. Their file has been indispensable
in breaking several difficult cases."

"Okay," Frank said. "We can catch a plane tonight and grab some sleep during the flight."

"What about me?" Chet asked.

"If you don't mind," Mr. Hardy said, "I'd like
you to stay here and lend me a hand."

"All right," Chet said. "But as long as we have
the details settled, what about that food we were
going out for?"

They went to a small Italian restaurant, and
after dinner walked back to the Seamen's
Haven.

While Frank and Joe looked for a taxi, Mr.
Hardy conferred briefly with Chet. The chubby
boy accompanied the brothers to the parking lot
where they had left their car. Next, Frank and Joe

dropped Chet and his suitcase off at Seamen's Haven, then headed for Kennedy Airport.

They parked and took their luggage from the trunk of the car. "I sure hope we can find some answers," Joe said as they walked to the terminal.

"So do I," Frank answered. "Blackright won't be wasting much more time on R. R. Dunn. There are a great many wealthy art collectors in this country, and unfortunately, not all of them are as scrupulous as Mr. Dunn. If Blackright contacts one of them, the Ivory Idol may disappear forever!"

They checked in at the ticket counter and were told that the next flight to Los Angeles did not leave for another hour and a half. Frank bought tickets, had their luggage tagged and put on the conveyor belt, then walked with Joe into the main lobby, where they bought two magazines at a newsstand. They found an isolated grouping of chairs and sat down to read.

Soon they were engrossed in their magazines. There was a rustle in the chair next to Frank but the boy did not look up. He was turning a page when a gruff voice said:

"Hello, brats!"

Startled, Frank discovered Mug sitting beside him! A quick glance revealed that Joe was flanked by Baby Face. Joe started to move, but Frank waved him back, realizing that if Mug and Baby

Face were confronting them in the open, the two thugs must have a pretty good trick up their sleeves.

"That's good thinkin'," Mug said. "You guys don't want to make a scene here."

"Yeah," Baby Face gloated. "Get up nice and quiet and take a little walk to our car."

"Why?" Frank's voice was cool.

"One, so your old man with his dopey dyed hair and his fake tattoo won't get hurt—and two, so your fat buddy stays just as healthy as when you dropped him off at Seamen's Haven."

"You see," Mug said with a sardonic smile, "our men are holding both of them. If anything happens to us, or if we don't come back with you two, then nobody'll see Daddy and Fatso again!"

CHAPTER XV

Tattling Tattoos

"Now, I want you to walk real slow and calm between me and Baby Face. Remember, any funny business and you'll be responsible for what happens." Mug stood up. "Come on."

Frank and Joe left their chairs and began walking with Mug and Baby Face toward the exit.

"You're going to pay for this," Joe said through clenched teeth.

"Wrong!" Mug answered. "We're going to *get* paid for this."

"That's for certain," Frank said. "But not the way you expect."

"Shut up!" Mug growled. "You guys have been a pain in the neck long enough and I don't want to hear no more out of you."

The two thugs directed the boys through the parking lot to a large green sedan. Baby Face opened the door in the rear and told Frank to get in. Baby Face followed the dark-haired youth, then ordered Joe to enter.

Mug went around the other side of the car and slid in behind the wheel. The big man lit a cigarette and stared idly out the window, smoking, as Baby Face quickly bound Frank's and Joe's wrists and ankles with stout rope.

"On the floor!" he said when he had finished. "Quick, move!" He pushed the boys down and threw a blanket over them. "Okay, Mug. Let's go!"

The car started off with Frank and Joe cramped, hot, and uncomfortable. "We really botched this one," Joe whispered. "We should have slugged it out with them right in the terminal."

"You know we couldn't, Joe."

"I guess you're right. But what if it was just a ruse? What if Dad and Chet are really all right?"

A shoe slammed down on Frank's back. "Shut up, you punks!" Baby Face grumbled.

"Aw, let 'em talk," Mug said. "It ain't gonna hurt nothin'. Besides, they won't be talkin' much longer!"

Baby Face seemed to find this statement hilarious. His laughter sounded like a high-pitched whinny.

"Frank," Joe said desperately, "if we don't think of something quick, we're going to end up on the bottom of a river!"

From the sounds of traffic, Frank guessed they were on an expressway. Mug drove at a steady speed for some ten minutes.

"There's the turnoff on the right," Baby Face said.

The car veered and a few moments later the sound of heavy traffic had been left behind. "That country road's only two miles from here, Mug," Baby Face directed. "Watch for an old scarred oak tree."

Frank and Joe had scraped their wrists raw trying to loosen their bonds, but to no avail.

"Here we are," Mug announced. "I'll go right past that deserted farmhouse, and if there's no one else on the road, I'll turn around, come back, and park."

"Good." Baby Face prodded Frank and Joe with his foot. "Say your prayers, punks, you've come to the end of the line!"

The boys were sweating. "Joe," Frank whispered, "we've got to hit them like wild demons when they drag us out of the car. Tied or untied. It's our last chance!"

"Right. We have nothing to lose."

Mug shouted suddenly, "Hey! What's that crazy cab doin'?"

"Look out!" Baby Face yelled. "He's gonna run you off the road!"

There was the tearing sound of wrenching metal, and the car came to an abrupt halt. Frank and Joe heard car doors opening. Noises of a scuffle followed swiftly and Baby Face was dragged cursing from the rear seat.

"Frank! Joe!" called a familiar voice.

"Chet!" Frank yelled.

The blanket was stripped away, and Chet Morton's anxious face peered down at them. "Boy, what would you do without me to get you out of scrapes?" he said, pulling his pals from the sedan.

Frank saw Baby Face shaking his head and trying to rise from the ground. Mug was wrestling with the driver of the taxi.

"Get us untied, quick!" Frank said.

Baby Face regained his feet and stood looking around groggily. Mug picked up a rock and hit the taxi driver on the head, stunning him. "Let's get out of here!" he shouted.

Baby Face needed no further urging. The two leaped into the car, and before Chet could untie the Hardys, it roared off.

"Man!" said the taxi driver, rubbing his head. "You told me it'd be rough, but I didn't think you meant getting clobbered!" He slowly scrambled to his feet.

In the taxi on the way back to the airport, Chet explained that the first job Mr. Hardy had given him was to shadow Frank and Joe to make sure they got off all right. Chet had seen Mug and Baby Face take his buddies to the car and tie them.

Afraid the criminals would be gone by the time he could get to a phone, Chet had jumped into a taxi and followed the sedan. He and the driver hoped to find a police car, but when they did not, Chet decided he had to go into action. He promised the driver that Mr. Hardy would pay him a reward for rescuing Frank and Joe.

"Great going!" Frank praised.

"Then Mug and Baby Face really were bluffing about holding you and Dad prisoners!" Joe said. "Were we ever fooled!"

Having only ten minutes to catch their plane, the Hardys thanked their pal and the taxi driver as he drove into the airport. They raced to the departure gate and made it with seconds to spare. After the plane was airborne, both boys fell into a deep sleep, awakening when the captain announced that they were landing at Los Angeles.

The Hardys spent the rest of the night at an airport motel, then went directly to the central offices of the Los Angeles Police Department, where they explained their mission to Sergeant Bill Thompson.

"Come with me," the officer said. "I'll take you to the files."

On the way through the corridors, the sergeant told them that most tattooing was a form of exhibitionism. Originally, tattooing had been done for purposes of adornment and beauty. It was an ancient craft—practiced by the Egyptians nearly three and a half thousand years ago.

Some people, like the Burmese and Maoris, had brought tattooing to the status of a very refined art. Tattoos, said the sergeant, could not be removed without leaving telltale scars and thus they were a good means by which to identify suspects.

The sergeant muttered to himself as he went through the card file. "Whale . . . whale . . . whale . . . Hundreds of 'em here." Then his eyes lit up. "Wow! Are you in luck!" He handed Frank a card marked:

WHALE, SOCIETY OF

Only a glance was needed to tell the Hardys this was what they were looking for. The society had been founded by a high-wire artist known as J. Kane. He was only five-feet-three and weighed a hundred and five pounds.

The names on the list found in the pocket of Meldrum's shirt, Frank recalled, were Pygmy, Blackright, Beluga, Blue, and Bottlenose.

"I think we can assume that Kane was Pygmy," Frank said. "Look here. The other known members of the society are listed as Tim Varney and Whitey Meldrum."

"Meldrum is Blackright," Joe remarked.

"Right. And Tim Varney, because of the post-card from Mystic signed *Beluga,* is our best candidate for Beluga."

"That leaves us Blue and Bottlenose," Joe went on. "Boko could be one or the other."

Thompson said he would have a photostatic copy made and took the boys to the police laboratory. Joe stopped short as they rounded a corner. He pointed to a Wanted poster on a bulletin board and exclaimed, "Baby Face!"

Quickly they told Sergeant Thompson of their encounters with Baby Face. He took down the poster and let the Hardys examine it. Baby Face's real name was Vinny Merks. His features were deceptive, for in reality he was in his late twenties.

Merks, who had served time in a Federal penitentiary, often posed as a juvenile. He was wanted in California on a variety of charges, and at last report was suspected of working with a former cellmate named Mug Stine.

The Hardys were exuberant over their discovery. When the copy of the file card was ready, they thanked the sergeant and left the police station. Since their return flight was not scheduled until the afternoon, Frank and Joe decided to go sightseeing.

"Where shall we start?" Joe asked, hailing a taxi outside police headquarters.

"Where the action is," Frank replied with a grin. "In Hollywood, of course. Maybe we can see some famous movie stars, too."

They asked to be let off at Hollywood and Vine. The world-famous intersection lived up to everything the boys had ever read about it, including two large groups of youths who took up positions on opposite sides of the street and began hurling insults at each other.

"At the rate they're going," Frank noted, "they'll be using fists before very long."

Joe was about to answer when he was seized from behind and dragged to a spot masked from public view by a truck that was backed up to a loading platform. As Frank spun to help Joe, a burly forearm choked off his windpipe.

Their captors were Baby Face and Mug Stine! Baby Face flashed a long, wicked knife. "Tell us where the Ivory Idol is!" he demanded. "Or else!"

CHAPTER XVI

A Phony Exposed

THE milling youths now provided an excellent screen for Mug and Baby Face, who kept their knives poised against the backs of the Hardy boys.

"We don't know anything about the Ivory Idol," Frank said calmly.

"Quit kiddin'. We read the papers, too."

"Listen, Merks," Joe exploded. "You'll never get away with this! That tattoo between your eyes is like a signal light and you know it!"

Baby Face was taken aback. "Where'd you learn my name?" he asked. "And how'd you know that's a tattoo?"

"We know about you," Frank replied.

"And the Ivory Idol," Baby Face hissed. "I'll give you three more seconds to start talkin'—"

"Dump!" Joe cried out. Frank instantly recognized the signal for an old trick. Both boys bent quickly at the waist, grabbed the ankles of their captors, and pulled hard. Mug and Baby Face lost their holds and dropped to the pavement.

"Into the street!" Frank shouted. They dashed forward the same moment the two gangs of young hoodlums charged at each other. *The Hardys were caught in the middle!*

They dodged, feinted, and ducked to get clear of the scene. Baby Face and Mug were not far behind, battling to get at them.

Suddenly sirens wailed and police cars and paddy wagons screeched into the area. Several of the youths bolted. A few got away, but most were caught within the police cordon.

Frank and Joe grinned as they waited their turn to enter the paddy wagon. "Just like in the movies," Joe said. "The cavalry arrives in the nick of time."

Frank craned his neck and looked around for Baby Face and Mug. "If we're lucky," he said, "the police will have picked up our playmates."

"All right!" said a big patrolman. "Into the wagon. Hurry it up!" The ride to the station house was short. The gang members were herded together in a large room to be booked. Frank and Joe, who looked out of place among them, identified themselves to the officer in charge and requested that he call Sergeant Bill Thompson at headquarters to verify their story.

Thompson came to the boys' aid immediately.

Hearing what had happened, he checked the list of prisoners. "Good news, boys," he reported. "Merks was picked up. Unfortunately Stine got away."

"Too bad," Joe said.

"Well, your job may be a bit easier now that Merks is out of the running," Thompson said. "Come on. I'll drive you to the airport."

He stayed with the Hardys until they boarded their flight. Soon after they were airborne, Frank pulled the copy of the information card on the Society of the Whale Tattoo from his pocket. He and Joe studied it carefully.

Mug and Baby Face, the boys concluded, were not in the society. Neither of them had the proper whale tattoo. Apparently they were independents hired by the society.

"Our first real response," Joe said, "came when we planted the story about knowing where the missing whale was. From that time on, we've been shadowed pretty closely."

"Right. But what about those thugs insisting that we know the location of the Ivory Idol?"

"Frank, I've got it!" Joe slammed his fist on the armrest. "Remember Merks' remark 'We read the papers, too'!"

"The Ivory Idol is in the whale!" Frank interrupted excitedly. "I should've guessed it before now. Kane must have hidden it there before he was killed."

"It makes sense! We've got to find the whale—and fast!"

It was late in the evening when the Hardys finally reached their home. Their mother and Aunt Gertrude welcomed them warmly and prepared hot chocolate and a tasty snack. As they relaxed, Frank and Joe related their adventures, including their search for Zelemeyer's Circus. But they toned down the more dangerous parts.

"Well, that's not *quite* the same version Chet told us," Mrs. Hardy said with a twinkle in her eyes. "But I suppose it's close enough."

"Chet's back in Bayport?" Frank asked.

"Yes. Your father felt he could form a new cover much better without Chet. But he's still working on your case, asking everybody about Zelemeyer's Circus."

"That's a good thought," Frank nodded. "Maybe Zelemeyer's did play in Bayport."

"Gracious," Aunt Gertrude said, "I meant to tell Chet about Mrs. Hendricks. She went to every one of them before her arthritis got so bad."

"Went to every what?" Joe asked.

"Circus, of course," his aunt replied.

"Sort of a circus nut, you'd call her, I guess," Mrs. Hardy said, and the boys looked in surprise at their mother.

"Well"—Mrs. Hardy looked embarrassed—"you can't live around two teen-agers without picking up some of their language."

Her sons laughed, and Frank said, "How do we contact Mrs. Hendricks?"

Miss Hardy went to the telephone, dialed a number, and handed the receiver to Frank.

"Oh, hello," Frank said to the pleasant though somewhat quavering voice of the woman who answered. "I'm Frank Hardy. . . . She's fine. . . . My mother, too. . . . No, nothing's wrong. I wonder if you remember a certain circus in town."

Frank explained, and as he listened to Mrs. Hendricks's reply, his eyebrows lifted. "Yes, go on, please. . . . And you remember a whale? Now, Mrs. Hendricks, please tell me all you can recall."

After listening a few minutes longer, Frank thanked the woman and hung up. Then he grabbed Aunt Gertrude and danced her around the room.

"My goodness, Frank! Are you mad?" she protested. "Careful of my spectacles!"

"For Pete's sake, spill it!" Joe cried.

"Okay. Listen carefully," Frank said as Aunt Gertrude flopped down in an easy chair.

The Zelemeyer Circus had played in Bayport many years before, at the old fairgrounds adjacent to the very spot where the new supermarket was going up. The circus went broke and disbanded. The stuffed whale they were exhibiting was buried on the spot because nobody wanted it.

"Wow!" Joe exclaimed. "What news! Cousin Elmer should hear this. Hey! Cousin Elmer!"

"Save your breath, Joe," Aunt Gertrude said. "Cousin Elmer is no longer with us."

The boys looked startled. "You mean he died?" Frank gasped.

"Of course not. He left. Flew the coop."

"That's right," Mrs. Hardy confirmed. "Elmer just upped and vanished two days ago without a word to anybody. We found a note on his dresser saying he was sorry he couldn't stay and meet Fenton." Their mother got the note and the boys read it.

"That wasn't very polite of him," Frank said.

Aunt Gertrude agreed emphatically. "Indeed not. And the way he ate my apple pie, you would have thought he'd say good-by in person. Not a true Hardy, that's all!"

"He might be the black sheep," Joe said, trying to make light of it, but the boys were instantly suspicious of the man who had accepted their hospitality.

"Anything missing around the house?" Frank asked guardedly.

Mrs. Hardy assured them that nothing had been stolen, and none of Fenton Hardy's records and files had been disturbed.

Frank was still not convinced. "There's something fishy about the whole deal—the way he came early, the way he wouldn't give any details about his past, and now his sudden disappearance."

"But the motive's missing," Joe said. "If he was an impostor, he'd have to have a reason."

"I'm sure he did. It's just that we can't see— Wait a minute!" He looked again at the note Elmer had left, then said, "Joe, do we still have that scrap we saved from the burning of Boko's strongbox papers?"

"Sure."

Joe went to their room to get it and Frank compared the two. "Oh, no! Our guest was none other than Boko the Clown! That sprained arm in the sling was a dodge to hide his whale tattoo!"

CHAPTER XVII

Rembrandt's Confession

No doubt about it. The writing on the two pieces of paper was identical.

"Oh! That—that terrible man!" Aunt Gertrude wailed. "To think we were living under the same roof with a criminal!"

"Well, he's gone now," Mrs. Hardy said. "He probably was scared that Cousin Elmer would arrive."

"We've got to find him," Frank declared. "He may well have the key to our mystery."

The next morning, after doing some chores around the house, the boys started to Solo's Super Carnival in Newton. If the heat was off, Boko might have gone to his old haunts. If they were lucky, the young detectives might actually nab him, or at least learn something about his whereabouts.

The miles whizzed away beneath the purring wheels and the fresh morning air filled Frank and

Joe with a sense of well-being. But when they rounded a bend in the road, a garish billboard broke the spell. It read:

NEW, SPECTACULAR WHALE SIDE SHOW!
At Solo's Super Carnival
See with your own eyes
The world's greatest
rarity

The lettering was in an inverted pyramid and painted at each side was a colorful whale spouting a great white plume of water.

"So it was Solo himself who got the whale!" Joe said indignantly.

"I can't believe it," Frank said. "No one but an absolute moron would steal practically the only stuffed whale in the world and then put it on display just a few miles from the scene of the crime."

As Frank guided the car skillfully over the rolling countryside, Joe wondered aloud whether Boko's action had anything to do with their buddies' whale.

"We'll know soon," Frank said. "There's Newton up ahead."

The tents and fluttering pennants came into sight, close to the edge of town. Cars were already trickling into the dusty parking lot. The Hardys found a place close to the entrance and locked their convertible.

A familiar figure greeted them at the ticket booth. "Hi, Frank. Hi, Joe," said Knocker Felsen. "How're you doin'?"

"Pretty well," Frank answered. "And you?"

"Not bad. Listen, you guys, why don't you go right on in? Free, I mean, to make up for what happened the first time. I guess I was just plain jealous and I wasn't thinkin' straight."

"Thanks, Knocker." There was a thin trace of sarcasm in Joe's voice. "Your change of heart have anything to do with the whale?"

Knocker looked blank as Frank went on, "And how about Boko. When did he come back?"

"Boko? What do you mean? I ain't seen him in a long time. He ain't been around here, if that's what you mean." Knocker studied the serious expressions on the Hardys' faces and a smile came to his lips. "Oh, the whale? Is that what's eatin' you?" He broke into a laugh. "You haven't seen our new side show yet. Go ahead. First midway to your left."

"What did you make of Knocker?" Joe asked as they headed toward the whale side show.

"If he's hiding something he's sure putting on a great act," Frank replied.

The Hardys paid their money and entered the huge tent. "Hey, what's this?" Joe asked with surprise.

A variety of mounted fish were positioned along the walls—sailfish, tuna, groupers, a few sharks, and several other multicolored specimens. On a long board in the center of the tent was a stuffed dolphin, much the worse for wear. And over the dolphin was a hastily lettered, single word: *Whale*.

"What a con job that is!" Joe groaned.

"You're right," Frank said. "But no one can accuse the carnival of fraud because from a technical scientific point of view the dolphin actually is a toothed whale."

"Boy, that's stretching a point mighty thin!" Joe declared as they left the tent.

"To say the least, but that still leaves us minus one Blue Whale and one Ivory Idol."

The boys went to talk to Sid Solo. He was happy to see them again, but had heard nothing further about Boko. Still under the impression—as was most everyone else—that the Hardys knew where the missing whale was, Solo congratulated them on their sleuthing abilities. He readily granted permission to talk to his employees about Boko.

Frank and Joe questioned the carnival people for nearly three hours, speaking a few minutes with them between acts and during coffee breaks. No one told them anything they had not heard before. One of the last they queried was Rembrandt the Tattooed Man. When Frank asked him if there was anything he wanted to add to his earlier statements, Rembrandt stared silently at his feet. He would not raise his eyes to meet Frank's.

"Rembrandt," Frank pressed, "there is something more, isn't there?"

Rembrandt bobbed his head. "I . . . I . . . don't know how to say it. I . . ."

Frank laid a comforting hand on the tattooed shoulder. "It's all right," he said. Take your time and tell us in your own words."

Rembrandt shook his head. "I was frightened, that's why I didn't speak up before. It's not easy for a man to admit he's a coward."

"Frightened of what?" Joe asked.

"It's a gang, I think."

"Why would they want to hurt you?" Frank pressed on.

Rembrandt swallowed deeply, then said, "Boko was one of them. I overheard a telephone call he made. There was something valuable hidden in that whale your friends found. So far as I could tell, Boko's gang had stolen whatever it was a long time ago and was now trying to sell it."

"But then why did Boko disappear?" Frank asked.

"He was going to double-cross his gang. Some private detective was going to pay him for information. Well, the gang found out and came looking for Boko. He took off. Me, I was too scared to let on that I knew anything at all. I'm sorry, fellows."

"It's all right," Frank said. "We understand."

"I know I should have spoken up earlier, but I hope you can still do something with the information."

"We can," Joe said. "Your information helps us to fit some of the scattered pieces of this puzzle into place. It explains why Boko was arguing over the phone about money."

The Hardys tried to cheer the tattooed man, but when they left, Rembrandt was still glum. The boys went to a phone and called the Bayport Airport and asked that the Hardy plane be made ready for flight. Then they called Chet and told him they were going to have another crack at finding the missing whale. They asked him to stop by their house, pick up their binoculars, and meet them at the airport.

They were only five miles out of Newton when the music program they were listening to was interrupted by an announcer.

"News bulletin," the crisp voice of the newscaster said. "Learning that Frank and Joe Hardy returned to Bayport late yesterday, a reporter from this station went to their home to obtain a follow-up statement concerning Biff Hooper and Tony Prito's stolen whale. At the Hardy home our man spoke to Chet Morton, close friend of the young sleuths. Contradicting earlier reports, Morton said that the brothers had *not* yet located the whale. In fact, they were going to make another search by air this very afternoon. Neither Frank nor Joe Hardy was available for comment. We now return you to our regular program."

"Oh, that's just great!" Joe fumed. "Now they know we've been bluffing all along. That little announcement might just have blown the case!"

Frank pressed down on the accelerator and stepped up their speed to the legal maximum. "We're not through yet. Those crooks are going to redouble their efforts to find the whale, but as of now they're no closer than we are. We've got to beat them to the punch."

They arrived at the airport, parked the car, and found Chet waiting for them next to the blue-and-white, single-engine plane. He still carried his little black case, and looked terribly embarrassed.

"I'm sorry, fellows," he murmured.

"Ye cats, Chet!" Joe said. "Whatever made you spill the beans like that?"

"I didn't—I mean not actually. It was that tricky reporter. He started firing questions at me like a machine gun. I got confused, started to hem and haw, and zingo! He put two and two together and went dashing away. I couldn't stop him."

"Well," Frank said, "no use crying about it. Let's get into the air and start working!"

The boys climbed into the Hardys' plane, fastened their seat belts, and warmed up the engine. Obtaining clearance from the tower, Frank taxied down the runway. The light plane gained speed and was almost at the point where Frank would pull back on the wheel and ease the craft up. But suddenly the plane slewed violently to the left and ground-looped.

CHAPTER XVIII

Bird Dogs

FRANK cut the engine instantly and the plane's wild gyrations came to halt a few moments later.

"Joe, Chet! You all right?" Frank yelled.

"I'm okay," Joe answered. "What happened?"

"Don't know."

Hearing a groan behind them, Frank and Joe turned to see Chet, his eyes glazed, his forehead marked with a red splotch from a bang against the cabin wall. The Hardys quickly unfastened their seat belts and loosened Chet's.

"Don't move," Frank cautioned. "We'll get help."

The chubby boy's eyes were clearing. "No, no," he mumbled. "I'm okay. Just a king-sized head-ache." He probed his injured head. A lump was appearing rapidly. "Ugh! Lucky I'm thick-skulled. What'd they do—drop the roof on me?"

Sirens wailed. Two crash trucks sped across the

field to the stricken plane, their red lights flashing. They squealed to a stop and men jumped from the vehicles with fire extinguishers.

"My brother and I weren't hurt," Frank told them, "but Chet has a nasty bump on his head."

Chet insisted he was all right, but one of the men advised that he see the airport doctor. They helped him from the plane and into one of the crash trucks which then sped off.

First making sure there was no danger of fire, Frank and Joe examined the plane. Two mechanics arrived in a jeep to probe for the cause of the trouble.

"She just whipped off to one side and began ground-looping," Frank explained. "Felt as if I'd lost a wheel."

Joe bent down and inspected the left wheel. "In a way you did lose one," he announced. "This wheel is locked solid."

Frank examined it, too. Joe was right. With the help of the mechanics, the boys tried to push the plane ahead. Its left wheel would not turn.

"That's impossible," one of the mechanics named Hank said. "We checked the wheel bearings just yesterday. There was enough grease on them to keep it turning for a year."

Frank leaned closer and sniffed. "Joe, can you identify that odor?"

Joe shook his head.

"We haven't any proof yet," Frank said, "but

I'll give odds that this is sabotage. There are half a dozen acids which lay dormant until activated by heat." Frank reasoned that such an acid could have eaten into the bearings, causing them to freeze.

"We'll check it out for you," Hank said.

The mechanics lifted the left landing gear and wheel onto a dolly. Then they climbed into the jeep with the boys and towed the plane back to the hangar area.

While Frank and Joe waited for Chet to return from the doctor's office, they checked to see if they could rent a plane for the afternoon. They were disappointed that nothing was available except a helicopter—and neither of them was qualified to fly such a craft.

"That's just great," Joe said. "While we're stranded, those crooks will find the whale and then the Ivory Idol will be gone for good."

"Wait a minute," Frank said. "Jack Wayne has his helicopter rating!"

"You're right. Let's phone him."

Jack informed the Hardys he would be at the airport within an hour. Heartened by this, the boys returned to the doctor's office. They found Chet smiling.

"Nothing broken," he said. "But I'm supposed to take it easy for the next few days."

Chet was told of the proposed helicopter trip. He volunteered to stay at the airport and keep an eye on the Hardys' plane. "I'll keep a lookout for any suspicious characters," he added.

"We'd appreciate it," Frank said. "But are you sure you're up to it?"

Chet nodded. "You could do me one favor, though."

"What's that?" Joe asked.

"Bring me that black case I had with me in the plane."

"Sure. But what's in it? You've been lugging that thing around with you ever since this investigation began."

"In it, my good man," Chet said, "are the tools of an artist. All my scrimshaw equipment. You don't think I'd let little things like a stolen whale and an ivory statue interfere with my hobby, do you?"

They brought Chet his case and got him positioned just outside the hangar in which their damaged plane was being examined.

Jack Wayne had arrived and checked out the helicopter. When Frank and Joe were securely strapped into their seats, Jack started the engine, let it idle a while, then engaged the rotors.

The copter lifted slowly from the ground, skimmed a few feet down the runway, then shot straight up into the air. They were on their way. Jack freed one hand and passed an air chart to Frank and Joe.

"That line in black grease pencil," he shouted over the roar of the engine, "represents a direct route from where the whale was stolen to the point at which you found the balloons."

"That's one of the problems," Frank answered. "Joe and I flew over every inch of that route and we didn't find a trace of the whale."

"What are the red elliptical lines you've drawn in, Jack?" Joe asked.

"Now there's where we might have some luck," the pilot answered. "Taking into consideration the meteorological data about the storm on the night of the theft, those red lines indicate ways in which the weather balloons carrying the whale might have drifted off course."

"I see," Joe said. "So if we search along these routes we might find the spot where the whale tore loose."

"That's the idea."

The first two areas they covered turned up nothing and consumed valuable time. Joe was discouraged. "Cheer up," Jack told him, "we still have two more to go."

"What happens if we draw blanks there too?" Joe asked.

"We'll just have to think of something else," Frank said.

Fifteen minutes later Jack pointed down to a field bordered by a small stand of trees, beyond which lay a sparkling lake. "Somebody else seems to have lost something, too," he said.

Three men were covering the ground bird-dog fashion. "Let's go down and take a look," Frank said. He pressed the binoculars to his eyes.

Jack brought the helicopter lower. As it neared the ground, the three men looked up, pointed, then ran for the woods. "It's Tim Varney and Mug Stine!" Frank exclaimed. "And Rembrandt is with them!"

"Rembrandt!" said Joe. "Well, I'll be a cross-eyed monkey. He certainly had us fooled."

The three men disappeared into the woods. Moments later, several white puffs of smoke appeared from the shadows of the forest. Bullets pierced the helicopter's Plexiglas canopy near Frank's head. Jack Wayne sent the aircraft leaping skyward.

"That was a close one." Frank took a deep breath.

"We're out of range now," Jack said. He radioed the airport, giving their position and reporting the fact they had just been fired upon. Wayne gave the criminal's names to the tower operator and requested that Police Chief Collig of Bayport be notified immediately.

"Man, would I like to get my hands on Rembrandt!" Joe said as the helicopter hovered. "I'll bet if we examined his right fist we'd find a three-part whale tattoo. Who would have thought

Bullets pierced the helicopter's canopy

of looking for a thing like that on a man whose entire body is covered with tattoos?"

"I guess we all goofed," Frank said, and added, "Suppose we keep an eye on those birds until the police get here."

Wayne circled over the woodland, but there was no sign of the trio. Finally the Hardys decided it was futile to keep up the surveillance. Also, seeking out the lost whale was more important.

Frank turned to the pilot. "Jack, there's nothing we can accomplish here. The police will have to find those men by themselves. Let's continue on the search route."

"Okay by me," Wayne replied.

He manipulated the controls and the helicopter moved forward. Past the trees, they flew over a cabin at the side of the lake. A speedboat was moored at the cabin's pier. Wayne came down for a closer look. The place appeared to be deserted.

"I think we can skirt around the lake," Joe said. "The whale wouldn't— Hey! Wait a minute!"

The thought that stopped Joe occurred to Frank at the same time. "Do you think it might have fallen into the water?"

"Why not?" Joe said with excitement. "If the whale went down in the lake, that would certainly account for the fact that no one has spotted it."

"Jack," Frank said, "take her up and move directly across the lake."

The pilot complied. From their vantage point, they could see far down into the clear water. The bottom was covered partly by weeds, partly by sand and jagged rocks.

Near the opposite end of the lake, Joe shot out his arm and shouted, "Look!"

Below them on the bottom of the lake they spied the dark silhouette of the whale!

CHAPTER XIX

A Bitter Loss

"WE'VE found it!" Frank shouted. The boys pounded each other on the back and shook hands with Jack Wayne.

The pilot grinned. "Okay, super-sleuths, you've located the whale. But what do we do with it now?"

Frank scratched his head. "This chopper's not powerful enough to carry the whale back to Bayport, is it, Jack?"

"Not by a long shot."

"We can't take a chance on leaving the whale here, though," Joe said.

"I know what," Frank said. "There's a coil of strong rope behind Joe's seat. If we could rig it to the whale, we might have enough power to raise the thing to the surface and tow it to the shore."

Jack thought for a moment. "Yes, I think we

can do it," he said finally. "But how do we get the rope on the whale?"

Frank began unbuttoning his shirt. "I'll attach it. The whale can't be much more than ten or twelve feet down. That's not too bad a dive, eh?"

"I don't know, Frank," Joe said doubtfully. "That water's pretty clear. The whale might be deeper than it looks."

Frank stripped off his shirt and T-shirt, then removed his shoes and socks. "Well, if it's too deep, then it's too deep and we'll have to think of something else. But the Ivory Idol is almost within our hands and I don't want to take any chances—not with those crooks in the woods. Take her down, Jack."

The pilot eased the helicopter to an altitude of no more than a dozen feet above the water. The down blast of its whirling rotors chopped up the surface.

Frank shucked his pants as Joe unlimbered the coil of hemp and secured one end to the framework of the helicopter seat.

Then he poised himself in the doorway, the free end of the rope in one hand, his pocketknife in the other. Jack brought the helicopter another six feet nearer the water.

"Wish me luck!" Frank called.

"Go get 'im!" Joe cried.

Frank dived cleanly into the water. The surface

turbulence created by the rotor breeze prevented Jack and Joe from seeing more than a blurred light-colored patch as Frank swam down to the whale. Joe leaned forward tensely.

Frank forced his way down with powerful scissor kicks and sweeping strokes of his arms. The whale's back seemed elusive, remaining just beyond his reach. The water was deeper than he had guessed, but he did not turn back.

At last Frank touched the rough skin of the whale. He probed quickly and felt one of the hooplike metal strips that supported the creature's basic form. Frank plunged his knife through the skin first on one side of the hoop, then on the other.

By now his chest felt as if it were on fire. His body was screaming for air. But he inserted the rope into the first gash and pulled it out through the second. Then he let go of the rope and swam furiously upward.

Frank's head and shoulders crashed through the surface like the prow of a submarine, and he sucked in a huge mouthful of air. Water, chopped up by the helicopter, splashed hard against his face and into his mouth. He motioned for Jack to draw the helicopter off a distance.

Refreshed, Frank bent sharply at the waist and dived down again. This time he located the rope, tied two hitches in it, and surfaced.

He signaled Jack to raise the whale. The helicopter ascended carefully, moved directly above the whale, then went up again. Frank let the taut rope slide through his hands. He could feel displaced water rolling against his feet as the whale rose.

Slowly the leviathan broke the surface with a great whooshing sound, water rolling from its sides. Frank rode high on its back.

The youth sleuth whooped with joy. He looked up to see Joe leaning out the copter door and gesturing shoreward. The craft moved forward, its rotors protesting mightily as the whale was towed sluggishly toward land.

The great behemoth created a large wake. Frank waved one arm around his head like a broncobuster in a rodeo and kicked the whale with his heels.

After the whale was beached, Jack set the copter down nearby. The trio congratulated one another exuberantly. Frank dried himself and slipped back into his clothes.

"Where do we start?" Joe asked.

"Your guess is as good as mine," Frank said. "The statue will probably be toward the center. Let's make a slit down the length, from the head to the tail."

It took the Hardys and Jack a while to cut through the tough hide. Then they rolled it up a few feet, giving themselves easy access to the sodden mass of straw and excelsior inside. Digging it out was no easy task.

"It's a pretty big whale," Joe said, panting. "But if I hadn't seen it, I never would have believed how much stuffing it could hold."

"I know what you mean," Jack said, stretching to loosen his tired muscles.

"We're looking for an ivory needle in a haystack," Frank observed.

"A six-foot needle!" His brother shook his head. "And we still can't find it."

As they worked, the distant put-put of an outboard motor came to them from across the lake. They looked up and saw the fishing boat that had been moored at the other end of the lake.

"Oh, oh! That just might be our three friends," Joe said. He sprinted to the helicopter and returned with the binoculars, which he pressed to his eyes.

"What's it look like?" Frank asked.

"There's only one man in the boat, sitting in the stern by the motor. I can't make out his face, but he's wearing an old fishing hat and jacket."

"Can't blame him for being curious," Jack said. "I'll bet it's not very often that he sees a helicopter hang over the lake, then dredge up a whale and tow it to shore!"

The boys laughed. "Well, back to work," Joe said.

The three thrust their arms deep into the stuffing and threw great bunches of the wadding onto an ever-growing pile. They had cleaned out nearly a fourth of the whale's stuffing before they had any luck.

Rummaging with a stick, Joe struck something hard. "Hey!" he called. "Over here. I might have hit pay dirt!"

Frank and Jack rushed to his side. The three of them tore away stuffing in large handfuls. Suddenly they exposed something about the size of a man—only thinner—wrapped tightly in old canvas that was secured with rope. They removed the item gingerly from the whale and set it upright upon the ground.

"Easy does it!" Frank cautioned. Their faces were tight with expectancy as he cut the ropes and pulled away the canvas.

Jack shook his head in disbelief. The Ivory Idol, glossed with a slight patina of age and carved with a delicacy that could only have been born of genius, stood before them.

"It's beautiful!" Joe said with awe.

Frank whistled. "No wonder everyone wants it."

Their mood was broken by the sound of the motorboat. It was drawing near the shore very quickly.

Frank looked up and said, "I'll bet the fisherman has never seen anything like this before."

The trio took a few steps forward to greet the visitor. Ten feet from land the fisherman pulled his throttle wide open and the boat rushed onto the sand with a grating sound.

The next moment two figures leaped up from the bottom of the boat. *Rembrandt and Mug Stine!*

The man at the motor threw off his hat, revealing himself as Tim Varney.

"To the copter—hurry!" Frank yelled.

Frank and Joe picked up the heavy statue and moved toward the helicopter as quickly as they could. Jack Wayne dashed ahead of them and tried to start the motor. The blades spun weakly a few times, but the engine coughed and would not catch.

"Frank!" Joe gasped. "We'll never make it with the statue. They're gaining on us!"

"Set it down!" Frank yelled. "We'll have to fight 'em!"

The boys laid the statue on the beach and braced for the attack. A moment later Joe went down beneath Rembrandt and Varney. Frank dodged Mug Stine and rushed to his brother's aid. The dark-haired boy tripped over a root and fell, landing on his back. The last thing he saw was Mug Stine swinging a hamlike fist down at him.

Mug joined Rembrandt and Varney. Outnumbered, Joe struggled fiercely, but it was a losing battle. In the background he heard Jack Wayne's frantic radio message to the police. The pilot signed off, leaped out of the helicopter, and ran to Joe's aid. By the time he flung himself onto the criminals, Joe, too, had been kayoed. Jack, fighting bravely but alone, was no match for the attackers.

The victors were grimly silent as they tied the Hardys and the pilot back to back. Jack grimaced with pain as Tim Varney savagely tightened the bonds.

"That ought to hold you," Varney snarled.

The assailants picked up the Ivory Idol and carried it to their boat. Then they shoved off, started the motor, and headed across the lake.

CHAPTER XX

Settling a Score

FRANK regained consciousness a little after his brother did. "You all right?" Joe asked.

"Yes. But my head feels like a balloon."

"I know what you mean."

Jack filled them in on what had happened after they had been knocked out. "So," he said ruefully, "I'm afraid all our efforts were in vain."

"We were so close," Frank said angrily. "So close! I just can't believe it."

"Well," Jack said, "we did manage to get off two radio messages to the police. Maybe they'll intercept these rats and recover the statue."

Joe's voice was morose. "Maybe, but it's only a slim chance."

Frank snapped himself out of his depression. "There's no sense in sitting around feeling sorry for ourselves. Let's go to work and see what we can do about getting loose."

"That's going to be tougher than it sounds,"

Jack said. "I've been trying and I'll say one thing for that guy Varney, he sure knows how to tie knots!"

Jack and the Hardys bent all their energies to freeing themselves. They drew in great lungfuls of air and flexed their muscles, then exhaled and relaxed, trying to work some slack into the rope. They pulled and pushed against one another, but could not loosen the bonds.

The afternoon lengthened into dusk, and soon their only light was provided by the half moon that shone above them. Swarms of mosquitoes added to their misery.

"Ouch!" Joe exclaimed. "I'm being sucked dry by these miniature vampires. What's keeping the police? Do you think they might not be able to find us?"

"Now there's a cheery thought," Frank said. "No, they'll find us, but we'll just have to sweat it out until they come."

Exhausted by their efforts to escape, the three huddled as close together as possible in an effort to offer only minimal exposure to the insatiable mosquitoes. Some time later Joe saw flashlights stabbing through the darkness.

"Look!" he cried. Then voices called their names—searching, anxious voices.

"Here! We're over here!" Frank yelled, and they all joined in excited shouting.

The bobbing flashlights swung in the direction

of the captives, then advanced on the double. In moments Jack and the Hardys were surrounded by six state troopers, two of whom immediately set to work cutting the ropes.

"Are we glad to see you!" Frank said. "Did you pick up those thieves in a dragnet? Is the Ivory Idol safe?"

"I'm afraid the answer to both questions is negative," said the officer in charge. "We did the best we could, but on such short notice were spread too thin. They slipped through us."

Frank, Joe, and Jack were helped to their feet, stiff and aching from their ordeal. Never had the boys been more crestfallen.

Jack Wayne went to tinker with the helicopter and managed to get the motor going. Then he and the Hardys thanked the police, climbed into the copter, and headed for Bayport. On the way, Jack radioed a message to Chief Collig requesting him to inform Mrs. Hardy of their safety.

Everyone was glum on the flight home. Each was thinking about the lost statue. They found Chet still faithfully waiting at the airport.

"I heard about it," he said sadly as he packed his scrimshaw in the carrying case. "Rotten luck all the way around. If I hadn't banged my head, maybe I could have gone along and helped."

"Don't blame yourself," Frank said. "By the way, any snoopers around our plane?"

"No," Chet replied ruefully. "They were all after you, I guess."

The Hardys said good-by to Jack, then climbed into their car with Chet. After dropping him off at the Morton farm, the boys made straight for home.

The usually ebullient Joe slumped in the seat beside his brother, chin in hand. He was quiet as the car skimmed over the highway. Finally he said, "Frank, we ruined our record today. This will be our first unsolved case."

"Don't agree," Frank replied. "We solved it all right, just didn't win it."

"Like in the carnival, huh? Rang the bell but didn't get the prize."

"Righto. But try to cheer up. Your chin's dragging on the ground. Don't let Aunt Gertrude read us, or we're in for a lecture."

"Don't worry. We're in for one, anyhow. Look at these rope burns. She'll be sure to spot them."

As Frank pulled into the driveway, Joe spied a familiar figure through the living-room window.

"Great spoutin' whales!" he shouted, nearly leaping from his seat. "It's Dad!"

Frank braked the car with a jerk and the Hardys hastened into the house. Greetings were warm and enthusiastic. To their relief, Mrs. Hardy and Aunt Gertrude were out. Fenton Hardy was in fine fettle. He had captured Whitey Meldrum in

New York and turned him over to the police, then returned home.

"And now," he said, "my boys are back again." He clapped both of them on the shoulders.

"But we didn't do such a hot job, Dad," Joe confessed glumly. He and Frank gave a detailed report of their exploits.

Mr. Hardy's face grew grave. "Frank and Joe, I'm as disappointed as both of you that we didn't recover the Ivory Idol. No one likes to fail. But you did have it in your grasp! It was only circumstance that snatched it away from you. When all is said, I'm as proud as a peacock about the way you handled yourselves and the work you did on this case."

The boys appreciated their father's efforts to try to cheer them up, but the taste of defeat cast a pall over them. Joe asked whether the gang might fly the statue out of the country.

"That's very likely," Mr. Hardy said. "And after that, it's highly improbable it will ever be recovered. I know it's—"

"Holy mackerel!" Frank slammed a fist into his palm, then struck himself on the forehead. "I'm an idiot. Why didn't I think of it before?"

"Think of what?" Mr. Hardy asked.

Frank told him about the shack on the waterfront where Tim Varney, Mug Stine, and Baby Face had met.

"Remember, Joe? There were some extra articles of clothing, some bedding and cans of food."

"Right," said Joe. "You think they might use it as a hideout until the heat is off?"

"It's possible. After all, they don't think anyone knows about the shack. What's your opinion, Dad?"

Mr. Hardy thought it was definitely worth a try. Speed was of the essence, so they ruled out driving to Mystic. At this hour there were nearly no requests for rented planes and they secured one easily.

"Let's give Jack a call," Frank suggested "I'm sure he'd like to come, and besides, we might need some reinforcement."

Joe hurried to the phone. Jack Wayne, who had just reached his home, was eager to join them and said he would meet them at the airport.

After leaving a note for Mrs. Hardy and Aunt Gertrude, father and sons hurried off. Jack Wayne was waiting at the plane when they reached the airport.

Up they flew into the night sky, and after a smooth flight touched down at a small private field five miles from Mystic.

Locating a taxi in the middle of the night took half an hour, but they finally found one and instructed the driver to stop three blocks from the shack near the Mystic waterfront. Mr. Hardy paid the fare, then they moved in on the shack by foot, advancing cautiously and keeping to the shadows.

"Look!" Frank said. "There's a light seeping around the edges of the windows. Someone's inside."

"Your hunch just might have paid off," Fenton Hardy agreed. "Easy now. We don't want to give ourselves away. Is there another entrance besides the one in the front?"

"No," Frank replied.

They crept to the shack and peeped through the crack in the door. Frank spied a long object on the floor, wrapped in a white tarpaulin. His whole frame tingled. *The Ivory Idol!*

"Listen," said Mug Stine's voice. "If we dump this baggage in the sea, no one will be the wiser."

"It's okay by me," Rembrandt agreed. "How about you, Tim?"

Varney nodded.

The Hardys and Jack Wayne pulled back a few feet. "We hit the jackpot all right," Joe said. "But I don't understand why they'd want to discard the statue. It doesn't make sense."

"There's only one way to find out," Frank whispered. "Listen, Dad. We've got a score to settle with those goons in there. If it's all right with you, we'd like to do it right now."

"Roger," Jack hissed.

"Go to it," Fenton Hardy said. "Clean 'em up!"

Frank and Joe charged the door and it flung open with a shattering bang. Mug, Varney, and

Rembrandt were stunned into immobility as the Hardys and Jack set upon them.

Frank's one-two punch toppled Rembrandt; Joe's flying tackle flattened Varney, and Mug failed to duck a haymaker delivered by Jack.

With a smile of satisfaction Fenton Hardy looked at the three men sprawled on the floor, rubbing their bruised jaws and glaring up at their captors. Joe dusted his jacket and said, "Guess you guys aren't so tough when the odds are even!"

The answer was a groan—but not from Varney, Rembrandt, or Mug. It came from the wrapped figure on the floor!

"Wh-what's that?" Joe blurted out.

"Me! Get me out!" came a muffled reply.

Fearing some kind of trick, Fenton Hardy handcuffed the criminals together, then bent down to unwrap the prone figure, which had started to wriggle. He split the tarpaulin with a knife and rolled the prisoner out.

Boko the Clown!

"Good night!" Frank exclaimed. "They were going to dump *him* into the sea!"

"We should have!" Varney grumbled.

"Quiet!" Fenton Hardy ordered. "Now tell us your story, Boko!"

Shaking with fright, Boko showered the Hardys with gratitude before revealing his bizarre tale.

He was Bottlenose in the Society of the Whale

Tattoo, and Rembrandt was Blue. Kane, who was Pygmy, had hidden the Ivory Idol in the whale owned by Zelemeyer's Circus, where he worked, because it was too hot to sell. When Zelemeyer had gone bankrupt, the whale was buried and Kane died before he could divulge its location to the society.

"When your friends dug up the whale," Boko explained, "something had to be done."

It was Rembrandt, however, not Boko, who was the informer. He believed the statue was still too hot to sell, so he decided to turn stool pigeon and make some money for himself.

The tattooed man glowered. He was the one who had entered Boko's bunk wagon and burned the contents of the strongbox.

"I knew he was after me and I had to get out," Boko continued. "I remembered the picture you boys had of Elmer Hardy, so I decided to move into your house as him."

"But why did you take off so suddenly?" Frank inquired.

"Well, the real Elmer Hardy was due soon," Boko said, "and besides, since the carnival had moved, I felt safer."

The clown was kidnapped, however, soon after he left the Hardy home. Rembrandt convinced Mug and Varney that Boko was the informer and they decided to silence him once and for all.

"They almost got away with it," Boko concluded.

Mug Stine and Tim Varney were just as surprised as the Hardys and started yelling at Rembrandt.

Joe interrupted them. "Never mind that now. We're not finished yet." Turning to the tattooed man, he said, "You were the one who put me on the Ferris wheel, weren't you?"

"What else was I supposed to do with a nosy brat?" Rembrandt retorted.

"What about the whale? You couldn't have carried that off by yourself with those weather balloons," Frank questioned.

"Whitey and Tim lent me a hand, and Baby Face . . ." His voice trailed off.

"And of course you had to knock Tony out to get to the whale," Joe figured.

Rembrandt shrugged.

Mr. Hardy turned to Mug Stine. "How did you happen to be at Kennedy Airport when Frank and Joe were waiting for their plane?"

Mug sneered, "We've been watching 'em ever since they left Mystic and went to New York."

Joe grew impatient. "Where's the Ivory Idol?" he demanded.

"Lashed beneath their rowboat," Boko revealed. "It's moored outside."

"Show us the place," commanded Mr. Hardy,

and asked Jack Wayne to stay with the prisoners, who again started arguing among themselves.

Using their flashlights, the Hardys and Boko reached the harbor side, where small waves leaped against a dory tied to a wooden dock. Stout ropes fastened to the oarlocks disappeared beneath the boat. Frank and Joe pulled off their shoes and trousers and jumped into the water, which was only chest high.

"I feel it!" Joe cried triumphantly.

"Me too," Frank said on the other side of the boat.

Inside the dory, Mr. Hardy and Boko quickly untied the knots.

"Okay, Frank. Got her?"

"Right!"

The boys eased the treasure to the dock where their father and Boko lent a hand to pull the magnificent ivory figure up to safety.

Joe grinned. "I guess we didn't lose our case after all, eh, Frank?" he said.

With the criminals and the Ivory Idol safely in the hands of the Mystic police, the Hardys and Jack returned to Bayport. Shortly after daybreak, Mrs. Hardy and Aunt Gertrude were awakened by lively banter as Mr. Hardy and the boys entered the house.

After a hearty breakfast the three detectives turned in and slept soundly until past noontime.

Chet, meantime, arrived at the Hardy home

and was delighted to hear that a big victory party had been planned for that evening. It would include Biff, Tony, Callie, Iola, and other friends of the Hardys.

Mrs. Hardy and Aunt Gertrude scurried about all afternoon preparing for the feast. When the guests were all gathered in the living room, they insisted that Frank and Joe relate the events of the past twenty-four hours.

In the middle of the party, Chet Morton stood up and asked for silence so that he could make an announcement. He said he had just put the finishing touch on a piece of scrimshaw which he now presented to Aunt Gertrude. It was an ivory instrument of delicate, symmetrical design. One end had three long tines and the other had a revolving wheel with a toothed rim.

"Oh, it's lovely, Chet! Thank you so much," Miss Hardy said. "But what is it?"

"It's called a jagging wheel and you use it for ruffling and marking the edges of pies."

"Are you trying to tell me something, young man?"

"Only that I hope you use it very often!"

At Chet's remark Frank and Joe burst into laughter, totally unaware that at that moment a sinister plot was brewing for them in *The Arctic Patrol Mystery*.

Suddenly the doorbell rang. Mrs. Hardy went to answer it. She returned with a man whose skin was weather-tanned, whose head was topped with a shock of sandy hair, and whose cheeks were covered with a full, flowing beard.

"I . . . I'd like to introduce Elmer Hardy to you," she said in a faltering voice.

Frank and Joe looked blank for a moment, then Frank grinned. "I can't believe it. Our *real* cousin!"

Elmer Hardy stared at them in bewilderment. "I beg your pardon?"

Frank chuckled, strode forward, and shook the man's hand. "I'm delighted to meet you, Cousin Elmer. Come sit down and I'll explain everything to you. It's a *whale* of a story!"

Order Form
Own the original 56 thrilling
NANCY DREW MYSTERY STORIES®

In *hardcover* at your local bookseller OR
simply mail in this handy order coupon and start your collection today!

Please send me the following Nancy Drew titles I've checked below.
All Books Priced @ $5.99

AVOID DELAYS   Please Print Order Form Clearly

❑ 1 Secret of the Old Clock	448-09501-7
❑ 2 Hidden Staircase	448-09502-5
❑ 3 Bungalow Mystery	448-09503-3
❑ 4 Mystery at Lilac Inn	448-09504-1
❑ 5 Secret of Shadow Ranch	448-09505-X
❑ 6 Secret of Red Gate Farm	448-09506-8
❑ 7 Clue in the Diary	448-09507-6
❑ 8 Nancy's Mysterious Letter	448-09508-4
❑ 9 The Sign of the Twisted Candles	448-09509-2
❑ 10 Password to Larkspur Lane	448-09510-6
❑ 11 Clue of the Broken Locket	448-09511-4
❑ 12 The Message in the Hollow Oak	448-09512-2
❑ 13 Mystery of the Ivory Charm	448-09513-0
❑ 14 The Whispering Statue	448-09514-9
❑ 15 Haunted Bridge	448-09515-7
❑ 16 Clue of the Tapping Heels	448-09516-5
❑ 17 Mystery of the Brass-Bound Trunk	448-09517-3
❑ 18 Mystery at Moss-Covered Mansion	448-09518-1
❑ 19 Quest of the Missing Map	448-09519-X
❑ 20 Clue in the Jewel Box	448-09520-3
❑ 21 The Secret in the Old Attic	448-09521-1
❑ 22 Clue in the Crumbling Wall	448-09522-X
❑ 23 Mystery of the Tolling Bell	448-09523-8
❑ 24 Clue in the Old Album	448-09524-6
❑ 25 Ghost of Blackwood Hall	448-09525-4
❑ 26 Clue of the Leaning Chimney	448-09526-2
❑ 27 Secret of the Wooden Lady	448-09527-0
❑ 28 The Clue of the Black Keys	448-09528-9
❑ 29 Mystery at the Ski Jump	448-09529-7
❑ 30 Clue of the Velvet Mask	448-09530-0
❑ 31 Ringmaster's Secret	448-09531-9
❑ 32 Scarlet Slipper Mystery	448-09532-7
❑ 33 Witch Tree Symbol	448-09533-5
❑ 34 Hidden Window Mystery	448-09534-3
❑ 35 Haunted Showboat	448-09535-1
❑ 36 Secret of the Golden Pavilion	448-09536-X
❑ 37 Clue in the Old Stagecoach	448-09537-8
❑ 38 Mystery of the Fire Dragon	448-09538-6
❑ 39 Clue of the Dancing Puppet	448-09539-4
❑ 40 Moonstone Castle Mystery	448-09540-8
❑ 41 Clue of the Whistling Bagpipes	448-09541-6
❑ 42 Phantom of Pine Hill	448-09542-4
❑ 43 Mystery of the 99 Steps	448-09543-2
❑ 44 Clue in the Crossword Cipher	448-09544-0
❑ 45 Spider Sapphire Mystery	448-09545-9
❑ 46 The Invisible Intruder	448-09546-7
❑ 47 The Mysterious Mannequin	448-09547-5
❑ 48 The Crooked Banister	448-09548-3
❑ 49 The Secret of Mirror Bay	448-09549-1
❑ 50 The Double Jinx Mystery	448-09550-5
❑ 51 Mystery of the Glowing Eye	448-09551-3
❑ 52 The Secret of the Forgotten City	448-09552-1
❑ 53 The Sky Phantom	448-09553-X
❑ 54 The Strange Message in the Parchment	448-09554-8
❑ 55 Mystery of Crocodile Island	448-09555-6
❑ 56 The Thirteenth Pearl	448-09556-4

VISIT PENGUIN PUTNAM BOOKS FOR YOUNG READERS ONLINE:
http://www.penguinputnam.com/yreaders/index.htm

Payable in US funds only. Postage & handling: US/Can. $2.75 for one book, $1.00 for each add'l book not to exceed $6.75; Int'l $5.00 for one book, $1.00 for each add'l. We accept Visa, MC, AMEX ($10.00 min.), checks ($15.00 fee for returned checks), and money orders. No Cash/COD. Call (800) 788-6262 or (201) 933-9292, fax (201) 896-8569, or mail your orders to:

Penguin Putnam Inc.
PO Box 12289 Dept. B
Newark, NJ 07101-5289

Bill my
credit card # _____ exp.____

___ Visa ___ MC ___ AMEX

Signature: _____

Bill to: _____

Address _____

City _____ ST _____ ZIP_____

Daytime phone #_____

Ship to:_____

Address_____

City _____ ST _____ ZIP_____

Book Total $_____

Applicable sales tax $_____

Postage & Handling $_____

Total amount due $_____

Please allow 4–6 weeks for US delivery. Can./Int'l orders please allow 6–8 weeks.
This offer is subject to change without notice.   ..d # _____